"What are you doing here?"

"I'm here because I made a mistake, and it's time to right that wrong." Jana's eyes shimmered with unshed tears.

"Where's my daughter? Where's Lindsey?"

She bit down on her bottom lip, and the tears started to fall.

"Jana, tell me where she is." The longer Jana stood there, the more worry settled in Blake's gut. None of this felt right.

"Lindsey's sick." The words tumbled out quickly as she took another step toward him. "We need you."

The words hit him hard. He didn't know what to say.

He took off his hat and brushed a hand through his hair. Blake returned to what she'd just said. They needed him.

"Blake, please." Her words were soft, pleading. His daughter was sick.

"Where is she?"

"Don't take her from me."

"Of all the…" He saw tears rolling down her cheeks. Real tears. He knew she was hurting. That didn't undo the way his insides were tied up in knots. "You took her from me."

Books by Brenda Minton

Love Inspired

Trusting Him
His Little Cowgirl
A Cowboy's Heart
The Cowboy Next Door
Rekindled Hearts
Blessings of the Season
    "The Christmas Letter"
Jenna's Cowboy Hero
The Cowboy's Courtship
The Cowboy's Sweetheart
Thanksgiving Groom
The Cowboy's Family
The Cowboy's Homecoming

Christmas Gifts
    *"Her Christmas Cowboy"
*The Cowboy's Holiday
    Blessing*
The Bull Rider's Baby
The Rancher's Secret Wife
The Cowboy's Healing Ways
*The Cowboy Lawman
The Boss's Bride*
*The Cowboy's Christmas
    Courtship*
The Cowboy's Reunited Family

*Cooper Creek

BRENDA MINTON

started creating stories to entertain herself during hour-long rides on the school bus. In high school she wrote romance novels to entertain her friends. The dream grew and so did her aspirations to become an author. She started with notebooks, handwritten manuscripts and characters who refused to go away until their stories were told. Eventually she put away the pen and paper and got down to business with the computer. The journey took a few years, with some encouragement and rejection along the way—as well as a lot of stubbornness on her part. In 2006 her dream to write for Love Inspired Books came true. Brenda lives in the rural Ozarks with her husband, three kids and an abundance of cats and dogs. She enjoys a chaotic life that she wouldn't trade for anything—except, on occasion, a beach house in Texas. You can stop by and visit at her website, www.brendaminton.net.

The Cowboy's Reunited Family

Brenda Minton

HARLEQUIN® LOVE INSPIRED®

Recycling programs
for this product may
not exist in your area.

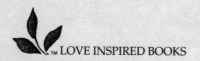 ™ LOVE INSPIRED BOOKS

ISBN-13: 978-0-373-81744-3

THE COWBOY'S REUNITED FAMILY

Copyright © 2014 by Brenda Minton

www.Harlequin.com

Printed in U.S.A.

But he said to me, "My grace is sufficient for you, for my power is made perfect in weakness." Therefore I will boast all the more gladly about my weaknesses, so that Christ's power may rest on me.

—*2 Corinthians* 12:9

To my lovely reader Tanja Cook Sedabres
for her help in answering questions.
Many blessings to you and your family.

And to my editor, Melissa Endlich.
I'm blessed to have you!

Chapter One

The big gray bull, part Brahman and part Angus, ran from the trailer. He stopped in the middle of the corral, snorted and shook his mammoth-sized head at Blake Cooper and his brother Jackson.

"He's mean." Jackson propped one booted foot on the bottom rail of the corral and leaned his arms on the top rail. "I'm not sure about him."

"He's at a level that most bulls aren't. As for mean, Jackson, there are no guarantees for a guy willing to get on the back of a one-ton animal," Blake offered, eyeing the bull that he'd talked his brothers into buying. He didn't usually get involved in this side of the business, but there were times a guy made exceptions.

He was the family lawyer and practiced law in the neighboring town of Grove. But he was a Cooper, and being a Cooper meant ranching was in his blood.

"I know there aren't," Jackson agreed. "I just try to stay away from the bulls that are pure mean."

Blake nodded because he couldn't have agreed more. They were in the business of raising bucking bulls, and both of them had been around long enough to know what a mean bull could do to a guy.

A car came up the driveway, swirling dust that would settle if they got more than a drop of rain. It was dry for May. Too dry.

"Someone you know?" Jackson stepped down from the fence to watch the car that pulled in next to Blake's truck.

"Doesn't look familiar." Blake adjusted his cowboy hat to block the sun and get a better look. "New York plates. Must be a rental car. Did you say someone was coming to look at that mare we bought from Wyatt Johnson?"

"Not until next week."

"Maybe just lost?" Blake offered, then he started toward the barn. He needed to take care of a few things, then head to his place.

Behind him, Jackson whistled low. "Blake, I think you might want to take a deep breath."

"Why?" Blake looked back to see what would cause him to need a deep breath. He would tell

Jackson later that a deep breath wouldn't have done him a bit of good. He wasn't even sure his heart knew how to keep beating. The woman, petite, blonde and rightfully hesitant, walked toward them. She didn't smile. Blake didn't feel much like smiling, either.

"Blake, I..." She shook her head and shrugged.

Jackson's hand settled on Blake's shoulder. "Don't go crazy."

"I'm not going crazy." He shifted his hat and glanced away from the woman standing there looking up at him with a million questions in her blue eyes. For a long moment he looked away, letting his gaze settle on the field, on cattle grazing, on all of the things he knew and he could handle.

"We need to talk." Her words were shaky and spoken with the softest English accent, the same accent that used to slay him.

"Talk? I don't know, Jana, maybe we needed to talk ten, almost eleven years ago." Blake looked at her, trying hard not to see her as the woman he'd loved, that he'd married. He needed to see her as the woman who had left him and taken their daughter with her. "What are you doing here?"

He needed to focus, to get his thoughts under control. It wasn't an easy thing to do. She was still beautiful. That was the last thing he wanted to think about her, not the first. Next to him, Jackson cleared his throat a little. Blake drew in a deep breath and focused on his ex-wife.

She shifted from one sandaled foot to the other, forcing him to stare at her pink toenails. He didn't want to notice anything about her. He didn't want to notice that she still looked a lot like the girl he'd met years ago in college. He didn't want to notice that her eyes were still as blue as the Oklahoma sky in March.

He wanted nothing from her but the daughter she'd left the country with all those years ago. He glanced past Jana, at the car she'd driven up in. He didn't see any sign of Lindsey. If he focused on his daughter, maybe he wouldn't get tangled up in Jana.

At that moment, Jana's gaze connected with his, pushing him off balance like an emotional avalanche.

"I'm here because I made a mistake, and it's time to right that wrong." Her eyes shimmered with unshed tears.

"Where's my daughter? Where's Lindsey?"

Jana bit down on her bottom lip, and the tears started to fall.

"Jana, tell me where she is." The longer Jana stood there, the more worry settled in his gut. None of this felt right.

"Blake, take a step back." Jackson edged close to him. "Give her a minute."

"I've given her ten and a half years of my daughter's life. Years I didn't have."

"Lindsey's sick." The words tumbled out quickly as she took another step toward him. "We need you."

The words hit him hard. He didn't know what to say, but he knew he needed a minute to process. He looked down at the hand that rested on his arm, the look in her eyes pleading for his mercy. He'd loved her. He remembered back to the woman he'd thought he'd spend his life with. She'd been a college student from England spending a year in America. He'd fallen in love with her soft gestures, her sweet innocence and the accent.

He took off his hat and brushed a hand through his hair. She was watching him, waiting. Jackson stood nearby. Blake returned to what she'd just said. They needed him.

"Blake, please." Her words were soft. His daughter was sick.

"Where is she?"

"Don't take her from me."

"Of all the…" He had to walk away. When he turned, she was still standing where he left her, tears rolling down her cheeks. Real tears. He knew that. He knew she was hurting. That didn't undo the way his insides were tied up in knots. "You took her from me."

"I know," she whispered, her gaze lifting to meet his.

Every emotion he'd felt in the past ten years rushed through his mind. The woman he'd promised to love "until death do us part" was standing in front of him. It was hard to look at her and not think about the past. She'd gotten tired of country life. She'd left him and taken their two-year-old daughter away from him, hiding her in Europe and then in Africa. He knew this because he'd been on her trail for several years. Yet she'd always managed to disappear just before he caught up with her.

The only thing she'd left him was a note telling him she couldn't be a Cooper anymore, and she didn't think he'd understand. Almost four years into their marriage, she should have known him better than that. He would have understood.

"Does any of this matter right now?" Jackson asked, jumping into the conversation, the voice of reason. "Jana, where's Lindsey?"

"Tulsa." Jana brushed the hair back from her face as she stood facing him, a lot braver than he would have been, Blake thought. "I brought her to Tulsa. She's in a hospital there. Blake, she needs a kidney transplant."

Blake was already pulling his keys from his pocket. He nodded toward the rental car. "You can park here. You'll ride with me."

"I can drive myself."

Blake laughed a little. "I don't think so, Jana."

"I'm not going to leave."

"I'm afraid I can't take your word on that. I seem to remember telling you that I had to make that meeting in Oklahoma City but we'd work things out when I got back. Problem was, I got back and you were gone."

Jackson interfered again. Blake needed to tell his younger brother that he could do without the kid gloves and worried looks. "Let me call Madeline and tell her what's going on. I'll drive the two of you to Tulsa."

"I can drive." Blake reached for Jana. She walked next to him, looking down, not up. He relaxed his hold on her arm.

"Let me go with you." Jackson stayed close.

"We'll take this." Blake opened the passenger door of the rental car for Jana. "Get in."

Jana got in. She looked up at him, her big blue eyes swimming in tears. "Blake, I'm sorry."

"I know." He closed the car door and turned to face Jackson. "Let the family know what's going on. I'll call you when I know more."

Jackson's mouth stayed in a firm line, unsmiling. "Blake, let me go with you."

"Not this time, little brother."

"Don't hurt her," Jackson warned.

"Hurt her? You mean like the way she ripped my heart out? Don't worry. I'm not going to hurt her. I'm going to get my daughter back and then I'll be done with Jana Parker."

"Blake, remember that the real issue at hand is your daughter. You're not thinking straight, and you've got a daughter who obviously needs you both."

Blake leaned back against the compact car Jana had rented. The reality of the moment hit him head-on, taking the air from his lungs as he tried to process that his daughter was back, but she was sick.

All of the years he'd dreamed about getting her back, he'd never imagined this scenario. He'd had it in his mind that they would reunite. She was always healthy, and Jana was never in the picture.

"Thanks." He managed a smile for his brother, then he walked around to get behind the wheel of the car. Next to Jana. He gave her a quick look and then jammed the key in the ignition, because looking at Jana did crazy things to him. After all these years he'd thought he'd only feel a serious dose of anger. But he was wrong.

* * *

Jana didn't know what to say to Blake. He got in the car, sliding the seat back to make room for his longer legs. She blinked away the tears that continued to fall. Tears that had been falling for weeks now. He had no idea how much it hurt, to watch her daughter suffer and to know there was nothing she could do.

That wasn't fair, though. He'd had his own share of suffering. And she was the reason why. Her actions had cost them all. It was time for making amends, for seeking his forgiveness.

She'd finally gotten it, this faith thing that was so important to the Coopers. She hadn't understood it when she'd been married to Blake. She hadn't seen the need for the Sundays spent at church and then together at Cooper Creek.

Now she knew what faith meant. She knew what it meant to face the past and seek forgiveness. But she couldn't tell Blake, because no doubt he would accuse her of using faith to manipulate him, to get what she wanted. She couldn't blame him for thinking the worst of her.

"What happened?" Blake's deep, husky voice broke the silence.

She glanced at him, at the strong profile she'd fallen in love with all those years ago. The first time she'd laid eyes on him, he'd looked like a model for a Western wear catalog. He'd been about to get in his truck, all cowboy from his hat to his boots. She'd been trying to start her car and couldn't. He'd come to her rescue. She'd never known a man like him, a man who wore masculinity the way some men wore cologne. It had been natural to him, to be strong.

"Jana?" He glanced her way, his mouth in a tight line.

"I'm sorry. I was thinking."

"Maybe you could tell me about Lindsey?"

"Her kidneys started to fail. The doctors call it Chronic Kidney Disease caused by a birth defect in her kidneys. She was weak, tired all of the time."

"Why wouldn't we have known that years ago?"

"Because she was young. Her kidneys managed while she was small. As she got older, her kidneys had to work harder and they couldn't keep up."

"What's the prognosis?"

"With a transplant, good. There will be challenges, of course."

"Okay, we'll get her a kidney."

Jana shook her head at his belief that it would be so simple. He didn't get it. They were here because she'd been on a donor list. They tried hospitals in Europe. They'd been fighting this battle for a while.

"Blake, it isn't that easy."

He clenched and unclenched the steering wheel, and she knew he was working through his anger. And his concern for their daughter.

"Is she on a list, and is she in a hospital that can do this type of surgery?"

"She is on a list, and this hospital has been doing kidney transplants for a decade. But the best donor is a living donor. A parent or a close relative is best."

"So we'll find a donor."

She nodded because she hoped they would. And she hoped his confidence would rub off on her.

"How is she right now?" he asked after they'd been driving awhile.

"She's getting stronger. Since we got here they've put her on dialysis to get her body healthier in preparation for the transplant."

"I need to know what you're thinking." He briefly looked her way and then refocused on the road.

"I guess my first thought is that we need to get our daughter better."

He let out a deep sigh. "I won't let you leave with her, Jana. I can't do that again."

"I know." She shuddered at the coldness in

his tone. He had every right to be angry. She'd known when she boarded that plane back to the U.S. that she would face his anger. She had known that returning could mean any number of things. But for Lindsey, she'd been willing to risk it.

"I want to know my daughter." He took off his hat and tossed it in the backseat of the car and brushed a hand through his dark hair, now touched with silver at the temples. "Jana, do you realize that something could have happened and I wouldn't have seen her again."

She heard the break in his voice. "I know, Blake. I'm here because I know she needs you. I know I've hurt you all, and I'll do whatever it takes to make that right. But please…"

"Please what?"

"Don't take her from me. I know you could probably have me arrested."

"I never pressed charges, Jana. It's hard to go that route when there wasn't a custody hearing. And I also didn't want the fear of being arrested to keep you from coming back with her."

"But you have the ability to take her."

"I don't want to discuss that right now."

She nodded in agreement, her heart slowly returning to normal. For now she could relax. She knew Blake, knew that they would handle one problem at a time. And the most important thing was their daughter's health.

"Thank you."

"Does she have any idea that she has family here?"

"Yes. I told her she has family in Oklahoma who can help us."

"Did you ever tell her that she has a dad who loves her? That she has a family who misses her?"

"Not until recently." She brushed a hand across her eyes. "I think she knew. She would question me sometimes, like she had some memories of being here."

"I don't even know what to say to you right now." Blake ground out the words. Jana shivered and hugged herself tight, wishing that she could take back every last moment of the ten years they'd been apart. She wished she could undo what she'd done to all of them.

Eventually she would explain to him what had happened to her. Now wasn't the time. The car zoomed along the highway. Jana looked out at passing fields, searching for the right words to make this situation better.

"I hope someday you'll forgive me, Blake. And I hope Lindsey will forgive me." She sighed and allowed herself to look at him.

"I can forgive you, Jana. I've had a lot of years to work on forgiveness. I can't say that I'll ever trust you again. And I definitely won't let you leave the country with her."

"Understood."

"I'll have her passport frozen."

"I know. Blake, I'm here. I know it will take you time to trust me, but I'm not leaving with her. If we can help her…" She covered her face with her hands as the tears unleashed again. "If…"

"Not *if.*" His tone softened and she felt a handkerchief being pushed into her hand. "We'll get her through this."

"I'm praying you're right."

"Oh, you *pray* now? I guess…" He stopped, sighed. "I think we'll both have to do a lot of praying."

"I want you to know her, Blake. I want to stay here so that you can build a relationship with her." Life, she realized, was precious. Her daughter deserved a relationship with Blake. With all of the Coopers.

"So, after nearly eleven years, I'll get weekends and maybe a couple of weeks in the summer?"

"Can you give me a chance?" She wiped at her eyes with the handkerchief. "Don't expect me to know every step we'll take from here. I want you to have a relationship with Lindsey. It's important. Life is too fragile to go on like this."

"You can stay in the guesthouse at the main ranch."

"Thank you," she whispered. "And just give her time. She doesn't know you. And before you say anything, I know that's my fault. But please, give her time to know you, to know your family."

They drove on in silence. Soon they were driving through the crowded, rush hour streets of Tulsa, headed toward the hospital.

"Does she know that you came to get me?" Blake asked as they parked.

"No. I didn't know what to tell her."

"You need to think of something. 'Surprise, here's your dad' isn't going to work."

"I know. She does know we're here because her family is in this area. She knows she's going to see you."

They got out and headed across the hospital parking lot, side by side, not touching. Even though his hand didn't reach for hers, Jana felt stronger just having him with her. She'd been alone in this battle for over a year. Having Blake at her side meant someone to lean on, even if she couldn't reach out to him.

He would help make decisions. He would be the strong voice she couldn't always be. And maybe, just maybe, they would be friends some-day.

Together they walked through the doors of the hospital, leaving behind the heat of an early Oklahoma evening. The cool, antiseptic world of the hospital greeted them. A lady at the desk smiled and asked if they needed anything.

Blake looked at Jana. "I'm assuming you know where we're going."

"Of course."

He followed her to the elevator. They stepped inside. Jana pushed the button and looked at Blake. She could see the pulse in his neck. As frightened as she was, she knew he had to be reeling right about then. She knew he'd searched for them. She knew he loved, had always loved, Lindsey. It had been her own selfish fears that had caused her to flee with their daughter.

She had to make it up to him, and to Lindsey. Regret welled up inside her and without think-ing she reached for his hand. She held it tight as she looked up at him.

"I am sorry."

He nodded. The doors opened. Jana led him through the corridor and to the locked door of the children's ward. Clowns and balloons were painted in bright colors, making it look like a happy, fun place and not a place where sick children fought to get well.

"I can't believe this." His voice broke.

"I know."

"She was just a baby, Jana."

She pushed the intercom and told the nurse on the other end her name. The door buzzed and Blake pushed it open. Jana remembered the only other time they'd gone to a hospital together. She'd been in labor. He'd been so excited. They'd been crazy in love.

They walked to the room at the end of the hall. The door to the room was closed. Their daughter was inside, waiting for Jana to return, and not knowing that Blake would be with her. Jana reached for Blake's hand. He didn't resist. She laced her fingers through his.

"Blake, she's small. She's frail."

He exhaled and then nodded. She reached for the door and his hand slipped from hers. As she pushed the door open, he removed his hat. He was strong again. He didn't need her to prepare him or to lend him strength.

They walked through the door into the darkened room, slivers of sunlight filtered through the blinds. The television played on mute. Lindsey—dark haired, pale and tiny—opened her eyes and turned her head to smile at her mother.

Jana watched as Lindsey's eyes widened. Her

mouth opened as she stared first at Jana and then at Blake. Jana's heart broke all over again as she soaked in the reality of what she'd done to her daughter. All those years ago she'd been scared and selfish; she'd made a decision without thinking about the people whose lives would be affected by her choices.

Blake walked toward the bed. "Lindsey."

Their daughter watched him, her lips trembling but forming a smile.

"I remember riding a horse with you." Lindsey whispered the words, then without hesitation Blake was at her side, gathering her carefully into his arms.

Jana stood a short distance away and watched as the strongest man she'd ever known held their daughter and cried. She had hurt him, and she knew that not being able to heal their daughter would hurt him all over again. Because that was Blake. He was a man who fixed things.

She knew that about him. Even after years of running around the world, she had known that Lindsey's greatest chance of survival would happen here, in Oklahoma, with Blake Cooper. For Lindsey's sake, Jana could face Blake's wrath. She could face what being near Blake would do to her heart.

Chapter Two

Blake held his daughter's frail body gently. She'd been a toddler the last time he'd seen her. He still remembered that day. He'd looked back at her as he walked down the steps of their house, heading for a meeting in Oklahoma City. She'd stood at the door and waved a pudgy little hand, grinning, a bite of cookie in her mouth and chocolate on her chin.

"I missed you so much, ladybug." He whispered the nickname against her dark hair.

"I think I missed you, too." She spoke with a soft accent. He remembered her voice. She'd had a Southern drawl, even on words like cookie. Now it was more English and unfamiliar to his ears.

Behind them, Jana sobbed. Blake didn't turn to look at her. He couldn't.

"We're going to get you better," he promised,

as he settled Lindsey back in her bed, pulled the blanket up to her chin and then kissed the top of her head.

"I know." Her voice sounded thin, weak.

"I mean it."

She smiled up at him. "I know that I'll be okay."

Blake's throat tightened at the look of confidence and assurance his twelve-year-old daughter gave him. She wanted him to believe she'd be okay. He would make sure she was.

He settled in the chair next to the bed, reaching for her hand. Jana took the seat on the other side, close to the window. She watched them together. Blake tried to ignore her presence. He couldn't. Somehow their gazes connected. More like clashed. She smiled a little and he nodded, trying not to be touched by that smile, by the regret he saw in her expression.

It was ironic, really. He wanted her to be sorry, to feel guilty. And yet he didn't want to believe that she meant it. He wasn't ready to think good things about her. He definitely didn't want to still be attracted to her. Leftover emotions were bubbling up inside him as he remembered how much in love he'd been with her.

Lindsey moved, drawing his attention back to the bed. She looked up at him, her face thin, her skin sallow in the dim light of the room.

She didn't smile but her hand tightened on his. "Why didn't you come see me?"

After years of searching for her, he didn't know how to answer that question. Did he tell his daughter that her mother had kept her from him? As angry as he was, he couldn't do that. He *wouldn't* do that. Jana would have to tell Lindsey the truth. It wouldn't be easy for any of them. But he wasn't going to be the one to turn daughter against mother.

"I think we'll talk about that later." He eased out the words, knowing it didn't make sense and Lindsey would question him. "Why don't you rest?"

She nodded and her eyes drifted closed. "You're not leaving?"

"They couldn't drag me away."

Her eyes opened again. "I'd like to ride a horse when I'm better. Mom says there are a lot of horses in Oklahoma."

"Yes, there are."

She squeezed his hand once and then her grip loosened and she slept. Blake looked up as Jana moved to sit on the empty bed behind his chair, closer to him. Too close.

"Have you told the doctors that she has family here?"

"Yes." Jana scooted onto the bed, sitting with her feet dangling, her hands clasped in her lap. "They'll have to test you to see if you're a match. Blake, it won't be easy."

"I know that."

"You might not be a match."

He nodded and looked at his daughter again. He had to be a match. "If I'm not, there are plenty of us. We'll find someone."

"What if there isn't one? Or what if one of your family is a match but they don't…"

He cut her off, raising a hand to stop the storm of words.

"Jana, someone will." He pulled his phone out of his pocket. "You do what you need to do. Tell the doctors. Arrange the testing. And we'll take care of the rest."

He got up and headed for the door. Jana followed him. Once they were in the hall, he realized she was about to lose it. She had probably been as strong as one person can be on her own. Now she looked like any strength she'd been holding on to was about to give out.

What could he do about that?

"I can't undo what I did." She leaned back against the wall and pinched the bridge of her nose with her fingers. Soft blond hair framed her face.

"No, you can't." What an understatement that was. She'd robbed him. She'd robbed Lindsey.

Come to think of it, she'd robbed his entire family. Lindsey's family.

Jana's shoulders started to shake. Her body sagged against the wall and her knees buckled. He grabbed her, holding her close as she sobbed into his shoulder. She still fit perfectly, and he didn't want that. He didn't want to remember how it had been when they were young. He didn't want her scent or her touch to be familiar.

It all came back to him. He pushed it away by remembering coming home to an empty house and a note.

He held her until her sobs became quieter, her body ceased shaking. He held her and tried hard not to think about the years he'd spent searching, wishing things could have been different for them, wishing she'd come back.

Before long, those years of wanting her back had been replaced by even more years of anger, of resentment, of not caring if he ever saw her again. All the while he never stopped wanting his daughter back.

"Mrs. Cooper?"

"She'll be fine," he assured the woman in the white lab coat walking toward them, her gaze lingering on Jana. "I'm Blake Cooper, Lindsey's father."

"Mr. Cooper, I'm Bonnie Palmer. I'm the

nurse practitioner handling your daughter's transplant."

"I'm the dad who hopes he's a match. Can an adult give a kidney to a child?"

"Yes, we've had great success with adult to child transplants."

He realized he was still holding Jana, his hands stroking her hair, comforting her. His hands dropped to his sides and she stepped back, visibly trying to regain her composure. She managed a weak smile.

"Where do we start?" she asked, her voice shaking.

"If the two of you could join me in the conference room, we'll discuss what needs to happen next for your daughter. And I'm glad you're here, Mr. Cooper. The sooner we can get this done, the better things will be for Lindsey."

Blake swallowed the painful lump that tightened in his throat. "Let's get started, then."

Jana looked up at him, her eyes still misty. "I'm sorry for falling apart."

"It's understandable." He shrugged it off, but not as easily as he would have liked. He looked from Jana to the nurse. "I don't want Lindsey left alone. I don't want her to wake up and think I'm gone."

The nurse indicated a room down the hall.

"You go ahead, and I'll see if we can find an aide to sit with your daughter."

Together Blake and Jana walked down the hall. He motioned her ahead of him into the conference room that was really just a room with more bad furniture that he barely fit in and a lamp to soften the fluorescent overhead lights.

The door opened and Nurse Palmer entered the room with a compassionate smile but cautious looks as she glanced from Blake to Jana. For thirty minutes she discussed what had to happen, and what were the best-and worst-case scenarios for Lindsey. Blake listened, trying to come to terms with the young woman in that hospital bed and the little girl she'd been the last time he'd seen her. All of those lost years. He glanced at Jana and she looked away.

"What happens if no one in my family is a match?" he asked the nurse.

"We'll continue dialysis and keep looking for a kidney. We'll continue to monitor her blood, her heart and her blood pressure. We're going to do everything in our power to get her well."

"And if we find a kidney?"

"If she's fortunate, she won't reject the kidney, and both she and the kidney stay healthy. Later in life she'll more than likely need another transplant. If she gets a kidney from a living donor we hope for twenty years."

Twenty years. She'd be thirty-two. Blake shook his head as the reality of his daughter's future hit. No matter what, she'd have a lifetime of medication and medical care. "So what do we do first?"

Nurse Palmer stood, clipboard in hand. "We can start testing you, Mr. Cooper. If necessary we'll test the rest of your family. If they're willing."

"They'll be willing. But let's just go with the assumption that I'm the donor. When would we do this surgery? How soon?"

The nurse smiled. "Let's take things one step at a time."

"It seems to me that time isn't something we have a lot of."

"Mr. Cooper, believe me, I appreciate the urgency of this situation."

"Okay, what's the first step?"

"We start with paperwork, of course. And then we'll do blood tests. We want to make sure you have blood types that match. The last thing we want is for her body to reject your kidney."

"I'm her dad—why wouldn't they match?"

"Mr. Cooper, being her dad isn't in question. Your blood type, the antigens in your blood and her body accepting your kidney—those are the issues we're looking at here. And we also want to make sure you're in good health and that you have two very healthy kidneys."

"Okay, let's go."

"Yes, let's." Nurse Palmer paused at the door. "Mr. Cooper, you have to understand this is a lengthy evaluation. It isn't going to happen in an hour. And it isn't going to happen today. We want a complete physical, blood tests, and we'll also have you talk to a counselor."

Great. They'd soon find out he resented the woman sitting across the room from him. He hoped that wouldn't undo everything.

"I understand." He reached for the hat he'd dropped on the end table. "But the way I see it, the sooner we get started, the better."

Jana followed them into the hall. "I'm going to stay with Lindsey."

Blake gave her a strong look and pushed back a truckload of suspicion. She wasn't going anywhere with Lindsey. Not now. He knew that, and he'd fight through the doubts about Jana and her motives. He'd do what he had to do to make sure Lindsey got the care she needed.

He'd deal with his ex-wife later.

Jana watched Lindsey sleep. The nurse's aide had left when she got back, only to return with a tray holding two plates. The meal was some type of chicken stir-fry. Jana tried to eat but couldn't. Eventually Lindsey would wake up, and when she did, she'd have questions. Jana would need to have the answers. Real answers, not the ones she'd given her for years.

As she had done for the past few months, Jana prayed. She'd learned to pray, learned to trust God. She knew that Blake doubted her. Sometimes she doubted herself. But she didn't doubt God or the faith that she'd learned to rely on when she first discovered that Lindsey's kidneys were failing.

She had termed it "end of the rope" faith. She'd been dangling at the end of hers, and God had reached out to save her, even though she'd always doubted His existence.

"You took me away from here?" Her daughter's soft voice broke into Jana's thoughts.

She looked at her daughter, at the hazel eyes that were so similar to Blake's. Those eyes were full of accusations.

"I did."

"Why?"

Jana couldn't look away from her child. She also couldn't avoid the answer that would make her look like the most selfish person in the world. But hopefully someday Lindsey would see her mother as someone who'd made a mistake and then tried to make things right.

For now she would tell Lindsey the basics, not

the whole story, a story that included not realizing how depressed she was during those dark days before she left Dawson and for months afterward.

"I was lost, Lindsey. I loved your dad, but I didn't know how to be the wife of a Cooper. I didn't know how to live so far away from London. I thought if I tried to leave him, he would take you away from me. I know that what I did was wrong, but at the time I wasn't thinking clearly."

"You knew he was looking for me. That's why we moved so often."

"Yes." The word cut deep, to the very depths of her soul. Jana reached to brush dark hair back from Lindsey's face. "I am sorry. I'm going to make it up to you."

"I'll never leave with you again. You can't make me."

"I won't try. We'll stay here so you can be near your dad."

"I want to live where he lives."

"Okay." Jana choked on the word, because she knew that her daughter meant living with Blake and not with her.

"Where is he?" Lindsey looked around the room. "Is he gone?"

"No, he's being tested to see if he can be your donor."

Lindsey reached for the cup on the table. Jana picked it up, held it to her lips. Lindsey took a long drink and then pulled away.

"Do I have other family here?"

Jana nodded. "Yes."

"Tell me about them."

"You have grandparents. Tim and Angie. I think Tim's mother, Granny Myrna, is still alive. And then there are about a dozen kids, your dad's brothers and sisters."

"A dozen?" Lindsey's eyes widened.

"Yes. The Coopers had several children, then adopted more. It's a very big family. They have a large ranch with horses and cattle."

Lindsey closed her eyes, a faint smile appearing on her lips. "I always thought I remembered my dad and the horse."

Lindsey opened her eyes again and her smile faded. "I'm mad that you kept me away from them."

"I know."

"Mothers make mistakes, sometimes." The woman's voice at the door startled Jana. She turned to face the visitors and then she stood as Angie Cooper entered the room. "You brought her back to us, Jana. That took courage."

Jana didn't know what to say. Behind Angie, Tim Cooper filled the doorway. Older, but every bit the man she remembered. He entered the room, frowning and then looked past her, his gaze locking on the face of his granddaughter, and he smiled.

"Lindsey, these are your grandparents." Jana stepped back out of the way. "Tim and Angie Cooper."

"You can just call us Nan and Granddad." Angie leaned over her granddaughter. "You are just as beautiful as I remember."

"I was little." Lindsey bit down on her bottom lip, staring up at the grandparents she'd been denied. Regret, Jana had so much of it.

"I'll be in the hall." Jana smiled at her daughter. "I won't go far."

Angie reached for Jana's hand as she started to walk away.

"Thank you for bringing her back."

Jana nodded and walked out the door. Her heart ached as she headed down the hall. She was fighting to save her daughter's life, but now she worried she would have to fight to keep her daughter's love, too. The Coopers were powerful, and even though they were kind, she knew they would band together to keep Lindsey close. And she knew, even though they would forgive, that they wouldn't welcome her back into their lives.

The doors of the hospital chapel were open. She stepped inside the quiet room with the wood pews and soft lighting, and for a few minutes she found peace. She kneeled at the altar, soaking up the presence of God, because she knew that only with His help would she get through the coming days.

She prayed for Lindsey. She prayed for healing. She prayed for forgiveness. Then she left the quiet sanctuary, not sure where to go but knowing she needed time alone, and Lindsey needed her grandparents.

"Mrs. Cooper, your husband is on the second floor if you want to join him," a nurse told Jana.

"I'm…" Jana paused, not knowing how to tell the nurse that Blake wasn't her husband. "Thank you."

She walked to the elevator. She hadn't planned on going to the second floor, but she did. After stepping off the elevator, she headed down a brightly lit hall. She saw Blake buttoning up his shirt as he walked out a double door. He was on the phone, telling someone he would see them soon and he would make it up to them. She didn't want to think about who he was talking to, but she couldn't help but imagine. It was a woman, someone he was involved with. Of course he had moved on. It had been ten years. She hadn't expected him to be alone forever.

He looked up, frowning when he saw her, then ended the conversation.

"How's it going?" she asked him.

"I'm finished with paperwork and officially checked in to the hospital, I think. They're going to run tests on my kidneys, heart and lungs." He shrugged. "They've already taken blood."

"Blake, I'm so sorry that you have to go through this. I'm sorry that we're pulling you away from your life this way."

"Why would you say that? Jana, I'd move heaven and earth to make sure Lindsey gets the help she needs."

She knew he would. He had probably moved heaven and earth trying to find them. Everything inside her ached when she thought about Blake's no doubt frantic search for his daughter. Not for his wife, though. He'd probably be happy if she dropped off the face of the earth.

Eventually she would have to tell him about the darkness, the depression, that had swept over her during those last months of their marriage. She would have to tell him how long it had taken her to climb out of that pit, and what it had taken to get her life back. But not now. He wasn't ready to hear that now.

"I know you would do anything for her, Blake. Thank you, for coming with me today."

"Stop thanking me. It makes me feel like a stranger who happened into your life. I'm not a stranger. I'm her dad." He pushed the button on the elevator. "I need a cup of coffee. Want to join me?"

"A cup of coffee would be nice."

As they rode the elevator down to the first floor, neither of them spoke. They were strangers, really. Jana didn't know about his life. He didn't know much about hers. They shared a daughter. That was it.

No, that was wrong. They weren't strangers. They'd been married. He'd wooed her, and she'd fallen in love. She hadn't exactly fallen out of love. She'd left him because she'd been young. She'd missed her home, people who sounded the way she sounded. She'd gotten homesick. Desperately homesick. And she'd grown terribly sad and hadn't been able to overcome it.

Now, almost eleven years later, they were back to being strangers. She didn't know the man he'd become. He didn't know her. She wondered if they'd ever really known each other. "I'm hoping that we'll know by morning if I'm a match," he offered as they walked through the doors of the cafeteria.

"That would be good." She followed him to the coffee machine.

He filled a cup and handed it to her and then reached for another cup. "Jana, we'll have to come up with a plan for sharing our daughter."

"She wants to stay with you," Jana admitted as she stirred sugar in her coffee. "She's angry with me."

"She won't always be angry," he said as he pulled out money to pay for the coffee. He smiled at the cashier, took his change and nodded toward a booth in the corner.

Jana waited until they were seated before she answered. "Won't she, Blake? Because I think she will. I think if I was her, I'd resent me. I'd want nothing to do with me."

"She's young. She's been through a lot."

"She's been through a lot because of me. So have you. I'm really kind of surprised that you would sit here and have coffee with me."

He was quiet for a long time, looking into the cup of black coffee, his brows knit together in thought. Finally he looked up. "Yeah, well, I'm a little surprised myself. I'm angry. I don't know if I'll ever trust you. But I do know that we have a daughter who needs us both. For her sake, I'll work through this and we'll find a way to be friends, to at least form a truce, because she needs that from us. She needs for us to be adults and pave the way for her to be happy."

"You're right."

"Am I? Because I'm talking about you staying here. The last time I saw you, you weren't too excited about living in Dawson. I still live there, Jana. And this is where Lindsey will live. This time I'll make sure you can't get her out of the country."

Her heart hammered hard against her ribs. "I'm prepared to do what I have to do in order to keep Lindsey safe and happy."

"You're prepared to live in the town you disliked so intensely you thought it would be a good idea to take our daughter and leave just a note on the table?"

She met his accusing gaze head-on.

"I'm not twenty-four anymore. I'm thirty-five. We've both gotten older and wiser. I've learned to deal with life better now."

If she told him more, he would understand, but she couldn't. Not now. Whatever she said would sound like an excuse, like a plea for sympathy. She couldn't tell him, not yet. No matter what he thought of her.

"Why didn't you come back?" Blake asked her.

"Because I didn't know what would happen. I was afraid you'd take Lindsey. I was afraid you'd have the police waiting for me."

"I wouldn't have done either."

"Are you sure?" She smiled a little, imagining what lengths he would have gone to in order to get Lindsey back.

"Okay, maybe," he admitted. "Maybe not."

He finished his coffee and pushed back from the table. "We should get back upstairs to Lindsey before I have to finish the tests."

The comment took Jana by surprise. She'd expected him to want more answers, more information. Instead he seemed to be done with her and with explanations.

She would survive his anger. At least she wanted to believe she would. But her heart wasn't absolutely sure it could survive another round of Blake Cooper in her life.

Chapter Three

"Mr. Cooper, you're a match."

Those would go down in history as the best words Blake had ever heard. He'd nearly cried when Nurse Palmer, their transplant coordinator, had given them the news.

Now, just twenty-four hours after Jana had showed up at Cooper Creek, he and Lindsey were scheduled for the surgery that would give her a second chance.

And give him a second chance to know his daughter.

Blake relaxed in the hospital bed next to Lindsey's. She glanced at him, shaking her head and then laughing. He shot her a look, trying to quell her mirth. Or make her laugh harder.

"What's so funny?" he finally asked.

She snickered again and the sound filled his heart. It had been empty a long time, he realized. In the years since Jana left with Lindsey, he'd survived but he hadn't lived. He'd worked. He'd somehow made it to family functions. It hadn't been easy, watching his brother Lucky's family growing, watching his other siblings marry and start families.

Just in the past few months he'd finally realized he had to do something with his time. That's when he'd met Teddy. He couldn't wait for Lindsey to meet the little boy that he'd started mentoring through their church program, which matched kids with adults.

He smiled at his daughter again and she laughed once more.

"You look great in that hospital gown," she teased. "And the cap on your head is perfect."

"They could make these things a little more decent." He made a face at her. "Or give me a pair of scrubs."

"Then you'd run around the hospital and act like a doctor. You'd try to do surgery or something."

"I think running will be out of the question for the next few weeks." The idea of slowing down didn't bother him a bit, not with Lindsey here.

It struck him again that they were having conversations, the kind he'd seen Jackson have with his daughter, Jade, and Lucky with Sabrina.

The last time he'd seen his daughter they'd been limited to conversations about cookies, puppies and going potty. Her laugh then had been babyish. Now she had a preteen giggle, and he was pretty sure she thought the young, male orderly was cute.

He would have to learn this business of being a dad to a teenager, to a girl who looked at boys. He'd have to restrain himself from hurting those boys.

"Where'd your mom go?" he asked after a few minutes of silence.

"Down to the cafeteria. She didn't want to eat in front of us."

Jana had disappeared while he'd been out of the room for more tests. It was easier to breathe with her gone. It gave him time to reconnect with his daughter, to learn who she was.

"Did you like living in all of those different countries?" he asked.

"Not all of them. Holland was my favorite. We stayed with a friend of mom's. A lady who was a flight attendant."

"Did you learn other languages?"

She nodded. "I speak German and Spanish."

"Do you have pictures, of yourself, I mean."

"On my computer. Mom can show you."

The door opened. Lindsey stopped talking. Her smile was hesitant. Blake glanced toward the door, expecting Jana. Instead it was his sister, Mia. She took in the situation. He held back a grin as she surveyed the room, his daughter and then him.

Mia bypassed him for Lindsey, her smile growing. "My goodness, you've gotten big. I'm your aunt, Mia."

"Nan showed me pictures." Lindsey offered her own smile. "You were a cop."

"DEA agent," Mia corrected. And then she smiled again. "Kind of the same. Are you ready to get this surgery over so you can come home?"

Lindsey nodded, but Blake noticed the look of hesitation. She didn't know what to expect from the group of people that had suddenly become her family. He had told her about the house she'd lived in years ago, about the land, the horses. She had few memories, obviously. The main one being him holding her on the horse.

"It's kind of scary to have this big family, huh?" Mia offered when Lindsey didn't answer. "Don't worry, it will get easier. I know from experience. I was eight years old when I became a Cooper."

"Seriously?" Lindsey perked up, intrigued by Mia's story. Mia had a way of doing that. Blake watched his sister lean in to share with his daughter.

"Yeah, for real. It was hard to get used to all of those Coopers. Sometimes I forgot to talk to people and tell them how I felt. So promise me you won't do that."

"I'll try to remember."

"Good girl. I'm always around to talk to. And your dad is always going to be there."

Yeah, that was the sister he knew and loved. Sometimes she withdrew when she had a problem, but she knew how to connect when she really needed to. She focused her attention on him, smiling big as she looked him over.

"What?"

She laughed a little. "Blue teddy bear gowns are definitely your style."

Lindsey laughed in response to his sister's comment. He glanced past Mia at his daughter. "Don't follow her example."

"Oh, you love me." Mia moved to stand next to his bed. "Do you know when they'll do the surgery?"

"They're waiting for results from one last test."

"Gotcha." She patted his arm, her new maternal side showing. She was a stepmother now to her husband, Slade's, little boy, Caleb. "Is there anything I can do before I leave?"

"Could you get that computer over on the table? Lindsey has pictures to show me."

"Got it." Mia grabbed the laptop and Lindsey fired it up. He watched as his daughter and sister looked over the pictures. Mia commented on a few of the photographs and then she picked up the computer and brought it to him.

"Thanks."

She smiled and shrugged it off. "Don't mention it."

Blake hit the slide show option and watched as his daughter's life flashed across the computer screen. All ages, all locations. But she always looked happy. She hadn't known what she was missing. The missing had been done by him. Mia glanced at Lindsey, then back at him. "She's asleep."

"She needs to rest."

"She's beautiful, Blake. And we aren't going to let her go again."

"Don't."

"Don't what? Be a good aunt? Care about you?"

"Don't be the family law enforcement officer."

Mia leaned close to his ear. "I'm being the person in this family with the common sense to know that Jana Parker Cooper can't be trusted. She came back for a reason. And when she gets what she wants, she'll leave. Someone has to be aware of that."

Blake lowered his voice. "Mia, I purposely never pursued charges because I don't want her to run."

"She *can't* run."

"What does that mean?"

Mia stepped back from him, a happy smile on her face. "Someone has to take care of you."

"I'm pretty good at taking care of myself. I've been doing it for a while. And I do things the right way, the legal way. Lawyer, remember."

"I try to forget that. It makes me itchy to think of you being a lawyer. You seem so normal and nice." Mia turned back to Lindsey. "That was a short nap."

Lindsey nodded. "I just get tired easily."

"So, what do the two of you do for fun when you're tied to hospital beds? I spent a lot of time listening to music when was in the hospital." Mia pulled an MP3 player out of her pocket and handed it to Lindsey. "All charged up and ready to go."

"Mia, if that—" Blake started, but his sister shook her finger at him. He didn't want to think about the fact that Mia had obviously just given his daughter something rigged with a tracking device. He closed his eyes and waited.

"That's great, Aunt Mia." Lindsey sounded as happy as any preteen.

The door opened. Blake waited, listening to

hesitant steps. Jana entered the room cautiously, glancing from Mia to Lindsey and back to Mia. "Hello, Mia."

"Jana."

"It's good to see you."

Mia smiled at Jana. "I brought Lindsey some music. I know from experience that hospital beds can be boring."

That triggered Lindsey's curiosity. "Were you in the hospital?"

"Yes, I got shot." She pointed to her right arm. She was still struggling to regain strength. The doctors had told her it wouldn't happen, but Mia didn't like to be told no.

"Wow, cool. I mean, bad that you got shot, but…" Lindsey obviously loved Mia. And so did Blake, when his sister wasn't in everyone's business playing detective.

"I really love you, Lindsey Cooper." Mia kissed Lindsey's cheek. "Jana, I'm glad you came back."

"Me, too, Mia."

Mia stopped in front of Jana, her jaw set at that determined angle she had. "I hope so."

His sister didn't realize it, but in her protectiveness, she'd pushed him to a place where he had to be the one to defend Jana, or to at least be on her side. He didn't want her to have any reason, any excuse to walk away.

* * *

Jana watched as Mia left, the door closing quietly behind her, and then she looked at Blake. "Well, it was nice to see Mia again."

"I don't think she likes you." Lindsey spoke, but her tone was distant, unconcerned. Jana looked at her daughter, who already was listening to music, a happy smile on her face.

"Thanks, I hadn't noticed." Jana sat down on the chair between their beds. For the most part the Coopers had been kind. Not exactly friendly, but kind. Angie had been the most welcoming, of course. Tim barely spoke. Jackson seemed to be on her side. Lucky seemed to tolerate her. Gage was busy with his new wife and didn't have much to say. Sophie spoke to her, and Heather had been willing to be a donor but hadn't wanted a cup of coffee Jana offered.

"Mia is always suspicious," Blake offered, his voice quiet but unaffected. "Law enforcement training, I guess."

"I'm not going to run, Blake. I know that I can't. And I don't want to."

"I'm counting on that, Jana." He glanced at his daughter. She seemed to be listening to music, but he saw her eyes flash with awareness in their direction. "Let's let it go for now."

Voices in the hallway drifted to their room. A moment later Nurse Palmer stepped into the room, a big smile on her face. Dr. Carver, the head of the transplant team, was with her.

"It's a go." Dr. Carver smiled at Lindsey and then at Blake. "You haven't been starved for no reason. We've scheduled the surgery for this evening."

Blake nodded and then shot his gaze to Lindsey. "You ready for this, ladybug?"

Jana's heart squeezed at the tone he used with their daughter. She blinked back tears as the moment hit her.

All of the months of worrying were about to end. She drew in a breath, but then she realized it wasn't true. The worry wouldn't end. There could be complications, rejection of the donor organ, infection. She knew every possible outcome. She'd talked to so many doctors. She'd worried so much.

A hand reached for hers, Blake's hand, bigger and stronger than hers. She looked down at the man in the hospital bed, the picture of health, of rugged masculinity. He smiled up at her, a smile that still turned her world inside out. Even after all of the years apart, it still happened.

"Don't worry," he said without a bit of hesitation. "I've got this."

She nodded but didn't trust her voice to answer. Nurse Palmer touched her shoulder, standing close to her.

"Jana, the emotions are going to hit now. I know this has been a long and difficult journey. I know there are still concerns and you don't know how you should feel. Take a deep breath and be relieved. There will be plenty of time later to worry more—" Nurse Palmer smiled "—but there will also be great times ahead for you and your family. Blake is a perfect match. He's a little older than we like—" she grinned at him "—but he has two healthy kidneys, and one of them will save your daughter. That doesn't mean there can't be complications, but it really does make things so much better for Lindsey."

Jana nodded again. Blake's hand on hers was warm and strong, sending his strength to her. "I'm good."

"We need to get these two prepped for surgery. We're going to move them in a few minutes. A nurse will take you to the O.R. waiting room. A social worker will give you updates."

Jana closed her eyes as her body began to tremble. It was all too real. The moment was upon them, and suddenly she couldn't be strong anymore. But she had to be.

"Jana, hug Lindsey. We need to go make a kidney swap." Blake's voice was light, casual. She opened her eyes and managed to smile, not cry.

"Thank you." She leaned, and still holding his hand, she kissed his cheek. "Thank you."

He reached up, cupping her cheek with his hand, forcing her to look him in those hazel eyes of his. "This is going to work. Don't lose faith now."

"I won't."

Slowly she released his hand and turned to Lindsey. The MP3 player was on the tray and Lindsey's eyes were huge, worried. Jana found her strength again. Right now she had to be Lindsey's rock.

"You're going to be healthy again, Lindsey." Jana hugged her daughter close. "You're going to be able to do all the things you love."

"Ride a horse?"

Jana laughed at that, "Let's take one thing at a time."

"Mom, I'm not afraid." Lindsey's smile grew. "I'm ready."

Jana nodded. Lindsey had found faith before Jana, and she'd led her mom to God. Now she said the words with a different meaning. She was ready for whatever happened.

"I'm going to be there when you wake up," she promised.

"I know." Lindsey cleared her throat. "I know I said things. I was mad. I'm still mad. But I love you, Mom."

"Oh, Lindsey, thank you." She hugged her daughter again, holding her tight.

"Time for us to go." Nurse Palmer put a hand on Jana's back. Jana turned and suddenly the room filled with staff that hadn't been there seconds ago.

"Okay. I need to tell Blake's family." Jana swallowed hard. Through the surgery they would have each other.

She tried not to think about being alone. She'd done this to herself. Tears clouded her vision as she glanced back at Lindsey and then at Blake.

Be strong. Be strong.

"Jana, we'll get through this." Blake spoke as she reached for the door. She wished she could say something, but her throat tightened and tears clouded her vision. She nodded and walked out.

We. The word stuck in her mind as she headed down the hall. She knew he meant that he and Lindsey would get through the surgery. But she needed to be a part of that *we.* She needed it, at least for today. For the next week. For the next year. She needed to be included in his life, in the strength that was Blake Cooper.

And once Lindsey had recovered, then Jana could be strong on her own again.

Chapter Four

Nine days after the surgery, Blake and Lindsey went home, to Dawson. The car pulled up the driveway to his house with Jana driving and Lindsey in the backseat. His family had said their goodbyes at the hospital, knowing the three of them needed to do this together, without an audience. They were going home, but they weren't a family. He didn't entertain any ideas that they would ever be a family again. But it meant something, to have Lindsey coming back to this house. Home again.

It meant something that Jana had brought her back, even if it had only been to get their daughter the medical help she needed. The reasons didn't matter to Blake, just that his daughter was back.

On the other hand, Blake wondered if Jana regretted that Lindsey's health had brought her back to a town and a way of life that she had never wanted.

The car stopped. Blake glanced back at his daughter. She looked a little dazed, a little lost. "We're home."

"Yes." Her one-word response came out in a whisper.

"Are you worried?" His hand paused on the door handle.

"No, not really. It's just strange to be here and to think that this is where I'll get to stay, that I won't have to move."

"You won't have to move." Blake looked from Lindsey to Jana. His ex-wife blanched a little at his tone. "Let's get out and see if things are still in one piece. Leaving Jackson and Travis in charge is never a good idea."

Blake pushed the door open and stepped slowly out of the sedan he'd talked Jana into driving. His car. His home. She hadn't liked the idea of giving up her rental car and using his car. Why should that bother her?

Jana and Lindsay would be living in his house, and he was moving into the apartment over the garage at Cooper Creek. That apartment would feel good after living in a hotel next to the hospital for the past week. He also planned on driving his truck now that he was home. A man could only be taxied around so much before it got under his skin.

His gaze caught and held Jana's as she stood looking at the house before opening the door for their daughter. He'd been gone a little over a week. She'd been gone over ten years. Nevertheless, they'd managed to forge something that felt like friendship. Or maybe it was just a truce. Everything he did at this point was for Lindsey's sake.

Jana opened the door so their daughter could get out of the car. He watched, waiting for her reaction.

It was a big moment, her first day back in the house she'd lived in as a toddler. He kept an eye on her face as he circled the car to help her. She glanced at him, then at the log-sided ranch house. Her eyes watered a little and she wavered. He reached for her hand. Jana stepped back, giving them space.

Blake spoke first. "You're home."

Lindsey nodded. She looked from him to her mother. "I don't remember it."

"You were a baby," he said.

"I was almost three."

He laughed. "Right, you should have had a car and maybe a place of your own by then."

"You know what I mean." She walked next to him, leaning close to his side. "I mean, I should remember. I remembered you. I wanted to remember this house."

He didn't know what else to say. He glanced back at Jana. She was pulling suitcases out of the trunk of the car and he guessed fighting tears. He saw her hand swipe at her cheek and he wondered, was she crying over the past or because she was stuck here?

He chided himself for being unfair. At some point he knew they'd work out a relationship that suited their new lives, as divorced parents sharing a child.

They reached the front porch. "Can you make it?"

Lindsey nodded but her grip on his arm tightened. He worried about her, probably more than he should. The doctors had declared the transplant a success. She already looked healthier, stronger than when he first saw her in the hospital.

Before they could climb the steps a loud bark split the air. Blake's border collie, Sam, came running around the corner of the house. The dog ran straight at them. Blake shielded Lindsey's body, but she was trying to get past him, making it hard to keep her safe from the dog that definitely wanted to jump on her.

Instead, Sam slid to a stop and sat down, his tongue lolling out of his open mouth. His black-and-white fur was coated in burrs. He'd obviously been in the field chasing something.

"Is this our dog?" Lindsey reached past him to pet the dog.

"Yes, this is Sam."

"Did you have him when I was little?"

"No, we had another dog. He was old." Blake couldn't help thinking about that dog, Bobby, and how he'd followed Lindsey everywhere. Jana had always been worried about germs and dirt. But Lindsey had loved him. Bobby, a blue heeler, had loved her, and if she walked a little too far away from the house he'd herd her back to them.

She'd had a dog, a cat and a pony, and she would have had cousins to play with.

As anger pushed its way in, he took a deep breath. Lindsey was petting Sam, and Jana was dragging suitcases up to the front porch that ran the length of the house.

"Let me help you." He gave the dog a warning glance before stepping away. Jana relinquished one of the suitcases.

"You're not supposed to carry anything heavy," she warned as she dragged the largest suitcase to the front door.

Blake took the handle from her. "Open the door, Jana. I think I can manage to drag a suitcase in the house."

She shook her head but she opened the door. She wouldn't look at him, but her hand brushed at her cheeks again. He followed her inside. It felt good to be home. The floor-to-ceiling windows in the living room let in the early-afternoon light. The house smelled clean. It looked as if he'd just been here. But he knew that the only ones who'd been here were his brothers, feeding animals and checking on the place while Blake stayed in Tulsa with Lindsey. And Jana.

He'd been released from the hospital a few short days after the surgery. Lindsey had been kept longer, to make sure there were no signs of rejection.

Jana had walked away from him. He leaned the suitcases against the wall and followed. She was standing in the dining room looking out the window, appearing to really enjoy the view of the Oklahoma fields.

"Jana?"

She shook her head but she couldn't face him. Her hand came up again, swiping at her cheek. She sniffled. He let out a long sigh, because he wasn't sure if he was ready to pretend the past ten years hadn't happened.

There had been times in the past couple of weeks that it had felt right, having Jana and Lindsey back in his life. Talking, sharing moments, and he'd thought that maybe they could go back to the way things were.

Then he'd look at his daughter, now almost thirteen, and he would think about all of the lost years.

From the front porch he heard Lindsey's laughter, the dog's high-pitched bark. Jana was leaning against the window, hugging herself tight as her shoulders shook.

His heart gave in a little. "She's going to be fine."

"I know she is. But—" she shrugged "—I did this to her. I took her away from here, from her family."

"She's happy, Jana. I guess you can't miss out on something you've never known."

She turned to face him, wiping away the last traces of tears as the front door banged shut and Lindsey called out, asking where they'd gone to.

"I hope you're right, because I don't want to lose her." Jana stepped past him, smiling at their daughter. "I think you should probably take a nap."

Lindsey's gaze flew to Blake. "I just got here. I'm not tired."

"You've had a long day."

"But I want to see the horses and the stables. Nan said I could come over when I got back."

"Right, and you will do all of that, Lindsey.

But not today. Today you rest." Jana's voice was strong again.

"What do you think, Blake?"

Blake didn't know how to step in, what role to fill. For years he'd been a single man searching for his family. How did he suddenly become the father? After years of parenting alone, would Jana let him take that place? How did a man step in as a father after years of being absent from his daughter's life?

His daughter looked his way, wanting him to be on her side.

"Lindsey, I think you should listen to your mom. As a matter of fact, I'll probably head home for a nap myself." He heard himself say the words with the strong, fatherly voice he'd learned from his own dad. He knew how the job was done, even if he was years out of practice.

"Home?" Lindsey looked from him to her mother. "Isn't *this* your home?"

Both Jana and Lindsay looked at him with questions in their eyes.

"It is my home, but for the time being, it's where you and your mom will stay. I'm staying at the ranch with my parents."

"Why aren't you staying here?"

"Because," he said, wondering if that was a good enough answer. He'd heard parents say it. *Because I said so.* Lindsey didn't look like a kid who would accept things just because he said so.

"Because…?" Lindsey looked determined, her chin raised a notch.

Jana smiled at him now, humor flickering in her blue eyes. Yeah, of course she was amused. He almost smiled back. And smiling was the last thing he wanted to do when it came to Jana.

"Because your mom and I aren't married, Lindsey." He saw the surprise on Jana's face. Had it never occurred to her that he would file for divorce?

"But you were. And this is your house."

"Yes, this is my house. It's a complicated situation, so for now we'll just deal with it one day at a time."

Lindsey walked away, back to the living room. She looked around the big open room and eventually settled in a chair by the window. He would give her anything. But he couldn't give her two parents who were going to live together. He wanted her to have what he'd had growing up—two parents, a big family.

"Lindsey, you have to understand." Jana sat on the sofa close to the chair where her daughter sat curled up.

"I do understand." Lindsey didn't cry but her voice wobbled. "I understand that I don't have a family. I understand that you might decide in the next few weeks that we're not staying here, either. Because we never get to stay anywhere. I'm tired of leaving places, and friends. Most of all, I don't want to lose my dad again."

Blake's thoughts exactly. He brushed a hand through his hair and sank into the leather recliner that he hadn't spent enough time sitting in. Come to think of it, he rarely spent time in this house. There were too many memories here. Memories of a marriage that had once been amazing, and then quickly over. All in a matter of a few years. He had memories of waving goodbye to his daughter, then of coming home to nothing.

He didn't blame Lindsey for her anger, for her mistrust. His gaze settled on Jana. She'd bitten down on her bottom lip and pain settled in her eyes.

"We're *not* leaving." Jana's voice was tight but determined. "I'm *not* going to do that to you again."

"But you didn't like it here before." Lindsey said the words he'd been thinking.

He remembered Jana telling him in the weeks before she left that she felt suffocated in Dawson, suffocated by his family and by church.

No matter how he felt about Jana, he could deal with it. He had dealt with it for years. He'd

managed to work past his anger. Now his job
was to help his daughter feel secure.

"Your mom won't leave, Lindsey." He sat forward. "She loves you and she won't leave. We
have to trust her."

He had to trust her. For Lindsey's sake. Because if Lindsey saw him trusting, she would
trust.

Lindsey looked from him to her mom. She
had the MP3 player Mia had given her and she
was fiddling with the cords. "Mom, I just don't
want to leave. Not now, not ever."

"I know, and neither do I," Jana leaned to hug
her daughter. "I promise."

Lindsey nodded, her eyes looking droopy,
even to an inexperienced dad. He smiled at her,
and she gave him a sleepy smile in return. But
he could see in her expression that she believed
her mom.

"I'm going to make coffee. Do you want a
cup?" Jana offered as she stood in the center
of the room looking adrift, not knowing what
to do next.

"I'm not drinking a lot of coffee these days."

"Right, sorry." She turned to their daughter
and Blake watched her face go soft. Lindsey
was already asleep. Jana pulled a blanket off
the back of the chair and covered their daughter. "I won't leave, Blake."

He nodded, because for Lindsey's sake he would make an effort to trust. But the difference between now and ten years ago was if she left, she wouldn't be able to take his daughter. She'd have to go alone.

"I'll get your water. Do you need anything else?" Jana stood in the center of the living room. The furniture was new and Blake had replaced the area rugs. He'd never liked the area rugs she picked. He'd told her then that they didn't match this home.

The rugs, like Jana, had been out of place here in the country. The one thing that both she and Blake had loved were the windows that soared twenty feet, giving them an amazing view of the countryside.

It was no longer her home. The little touches that had been hers were gone. The only thing that hadn't changed was their daughter's bedroom, with the twin bed covered in a quilt his mother had made. There were stuffed animals, just as they'd left them, and a dollhouse fit for a princess.

If she stayed in Dawson she'd have to get her own place. But first she'd have to get a job. The money left in trust by her parents was running low. She knew if Blake found out he'd suspect her of coming back to Oklahoma for money.

Nothing could be further from the truth. She'd used her money to pay for Lindsey's health care. She'd known all along that after Lindsey's transplant she'd have to get a job.

She'd buy a little house in Dawson. She'd attend church. She would make this community her home.

Blake's eyes were closed. She watched him for a moment, lost in thought. She'd always known he was a good man. Someone steady and dependable, a man you could count on.

For another few minutes she watched him in the chair, stretched out, his eyes shut, his breathing growing deep. Finally she walked away.

When she returned with the water, Blake was asleep. She pulled an afghan off the back of the sofa and draped it over him. She hesitated for a moment and then touched his cheek.

Oh, she was sorry, so very sorry. But she knew he wouldn't believe her. He would believe that she had needed his help for Lindsey's sake. He might even believe that she'd fallen on hard times and that had forced her to come running back to him. But would he ever believe how much she regretted leaving?

She moved her hand and shifted her attention from Blake to their daughter. She watched the easy breaths of a deep sleep. Jana had always watched Lindsey breathe. Moms did that. She was sure they all did. But in the past year she'd watched for different reasons. Because she needed to know that her daughter would take that next breath.

She'd spent a lot of time praying. For her daughter, for herself. She'd prayed about coming back to Dawson because she'd known that showing up in Oklahoma had several possible outcomes. Her biggest fear had been that Blake would have her arrested and she wouldn't be able to watch over Lindsey.

She would have gone to jail. To keep Lindsey alive, she would have done anything, even that.

As Blake and Lindsey slept, she slipped out of the house, needing a moment to clear her head. She walked toward the barn. The dog, Sam, fell in beside her. The border collie raced ahead, found a stick and came back. Jana reached for the stick but Sam pulled away, unwilling to let her have his toy. The dog plopped to the ground, his paws holding the stick as he gnawed on it.

In the fields horses grazed. A few cattle dotted the far pasture. She stood at the corral fence watching a pony chomp on tufts of spring grass. She wasn't sure, but she thought it might be the same pony Blake had bought Lindsey when she turned two. The little animal with the shaggy gray mane and darker gray coat looked up, watching her with an eager curiosity.

It chewed the last bite of grass and then ambled toward her. His dark eyes watched her, curious, intent.

"Billy Joe." She remembered his name. His ears twitched, and he shoved his velvety nose at her, wanting attention.

Tears overflowed her eyes. Blake had kept the pony for ten years, waiting for his daughter to return. She reached through the fence and pulled the face of the pony close, breathing in his horse scent. She brushed the tears away. The pony slipped from her grasp, more interested in grazing the fresh shoots of spring grass.

Jana closed her eyes, praying her family would be healed. This was a new prayer for her. She'd prayed for Lindsey, for a kidney and that Blake wouldn't have her arrested. She hadn't ever thought that her heart would still be so attached to the man who had been her husband.

Footsteps crunched in the gravel behind her. She waited, knowing it would be Blake.

"He's getting old," Blake said as he walked up. "But I couldn't let him go."

"I know." She swallowed and blinked quick to rid her eyes of more tears.

He cleared his throat. "I should have told you about the divorce."

"I was gone. You had every right to move on."

"I haven't really moved on." He looked away, leaving her to wonder about that statement. She wanted to ask why, but she didn't dare.

"Mia told me you had found us."

"She did, did she?"

"Yes. Were you going to take Lindsey?"

"I don't know." He stepped away from the fence. "Maybe. But I didn't get the chance. You were gone before I could get there. It was last fall."

"We were in Europe by then, looking for doctors."

They started back toward the house, the dog walking next to Blake. He pulled keys out of his pocket. "I'm going to head to Cooper Creek. Is there anything you need before I go?"

She wanted to tell him to stay with them, not to go. Lindsey would wake up and wonder where he had gone. Jana knew the right thing to do, even though it wouldn't be the easy one.

"You stay here. I'll go to the ranch," she offered.

Blake stopped walking. Instead of looking thankful, he looked suspicious.

"Don't look at me like that, Blake. I'm not going to bring my sick daughter to you and then leave town. I'm offering you the opportunity to stay with her. I know she wants to be with you."

His features relaxed. "She needs you, too."

"I want to believe that. But I don't know if she wants to need me right now. I knew that when I made this decision I'd have to deal with her anger. I knew it would hurt."

"She'll work through it."

"I hope."

"We all will." He stopped next to his truck. "We're going to have to sit down and talk about the future, and what we're going to do."

"Do you plan on trying to get custody of Lindsey?" Her voice shook. So did her legs.

"According to U.S. law, I have custody. My lawyer took care of that when he finalized our divorce."

Her hands went numb as she stood there looking up at him, trying to breathe. He could take Lindsey. Of course she knew that, but hearing it was another story. She closed her eyes and fought a wave of nausea.

"Jana, I won't take her." His voice, low and husky, soothed, even if that wasn't his intention. She opened her eyes and stared up at him.

"Thank you."

"She's going to have a long road ahead of her. I think for now we work as a team, not as a divided family. We'll go to doctor's appointments together. I think it would be good if the two of you were a part of the Cooper family."

"I don't want her to get the wrong idea. About us, I mean."

Blake didn't smile. She wanted him to smile. She wanted the tense lines in his face to relax. Time, she told herself. Everything would take time. She would relax and stop feeling like a cornered rabbit. He would stop looking angry. Time. Their daughter would feel secure in time.

"Maybe the best plan would be for us to sit down and talk to her," Jana suggested. "She's almost thirteen. She knows how life works. I think she has a good idea of what happened between us, and she'll understand that we're here for her. It isn't about us."

"I think that's a good idea." He reached for the door of the truck. "I've got something I need to take care of, so I'll be back in the morning. If you need anything, call my cell phone."

She nodded and backed away from the truck, from the man whose arms she might have turned to, had things been different.

Now she knew that she didn't have the right to reach out to him, to need him, to turn to him. She didn't have the right to question where, or who, he was going to when he left them.

"I'll see you tomorrow." She smiled, trying to make it seem easy.

He got behind the wheel of the truck. "Call. I'm just a few minutes away."

"I will. And you, too. I mean, if you need anything."

She stood in the yard of what had once been her house and watched his truck go down the drive. When she walked back toward the house, Lindsey was in the doorway.

"Where's he going?"

"Back to Cooper Creek."

"He didn't say goodbye."

"He thought you were sleeping."

Lindsey bit down on her bottom lip, but her eyes were foggy, and even though she looked better than she had two weeks ago, she still looked frail. Jana put an arm around her daughter and led her back to the couch.

"He'll be back tomorrow." She sat down next to Lindsey.

"I don't understand why he can't just stay here."

Jana sighed, because they were going to have to have this discussion now.

"Lindsey, we're here because I wanted you to know your dad again. What I did was wrong. It doesn't matter why I did it or what I felt at the time, it was the worst thing I could have done to you and to your dad. But your father and I are not a couple."

"But we're back." Lindsey sobbed the words. "We're back and you still love him."

Jana didn't answer. What could she say to that? Acknowledge that her daughter was right? Deny it because it would be easier in the long run?

She decided to change the subject. "What do you want to eat? Angie said she stocked the freezer, and there are plenty of good, healthy snacks in the cabinets."

Lindsey shrugged but Jana could see the wheels working. Her daughter was processing her new life, her parents' relationship. Of course she would eventually come to terms with the situation. Jana knew her daughter was good at adapting.

If only Jana had the same skills. Life would be so much easier if she could adapt to Blake being back in her life. He was a stranger. And yet, he wasn't.

He was her husband. Ex-husband, she corrected herself. It hurt, the way the truth was supposed to hurt. All of these years of being apart and her heart still wanted to claim him as her own.

Chapter Five

Blake walked through the barn at Cooper Creek, aware he wasn't alone. He'd seen Jackson's truck parked by the house, and since he hadn't seen him in the house, figured he must be out here. He checked the office and then headed for the arena.

Jackson was there, sitting on top of a horse that didn't seem to want to be ridden. Blake stood in the doorway, watching as Jackson hunkered down on the big red gelding. The horse never fully bucked, but he hunched a few times and walked stiff-legged like he had every intention of sending his rider flying. Jackson wasn't one to give up, though. He stuck it out, and eventually the horse relaxed into a somewhat easy walk.

That's when Blake stepped out of the shadows and walked around the back side of the chutes they used for bucking bulls.

Jackson rode up to the gate and dismounted. The horse shook like a wet dog and backed away from his rider. Jackson opened the gate and led the horse out.

"What brings you out here?" Jackson headed toward the exit door.

"I guess I live here for now. Shouldn't you be at home with your family?"

"Jade and Madeline went shopping. Mom has the little guy."

Noah, the baby Jackson and Maddie had adopted, was a cute kid. Recently they'd learned he might have siblings in Texas, placed in a group home.

"You still looking into Noah's brother and sister?" Blake wanted to talk about something other than his own family situation. Jana and Lindsey back in his life had been the thing he'd wanted most, or at least he'd wanted his daughter back. Now it was all about getting used to having them around again.

For years he'd been trying to get used to not having them.

For years Jackson had been the Cooper who didn't seem to have any interest in settling down, and now he had a wife, a daughter and son and maybe more kids on the way.

Jackson cross-tied the gelding and proceeded to unsaddle him. He gave Blake a quick look.

"We're going down at the end of the month to meet them. They were in foster care, but the foster parents weren't interested in adopting and it's hard to place siblings."

"How old are they?" Blake picked up the saddle and carried it in the tack room. When he walked back out, Jackson was brushing the horse.

"Six and seven. The mom lost them when they were toddlers."

"That's rough."

"Yeah, it is. Jade is all for adding to our family. Maddie is thrilled." Jackson's daughter, Jade, was adopted right after he and Maddie married. She'd showed up on Jackson's doorstep a couple of years ago, looking for her dad and thinking Jackson was the guy.

Blake guessed she'd been right.

"How are you feeling?" Blake asked, happy to focus on someone else's family life. "About adopting more kids."

Jackson grinned. "Pretty good. What about you? Why are you over here and not at your place?"

"I think you know the answer to that question." Blake stretched his legs and watched Jackson lead the horse down the aisle to a stall. "Where'd that horse come from?"

"I'm training him for a doctor in Oklahoma City."

"Nice horse."

"Yeah, not bad." Jackson closed the stall door and headed back to the bench where Blake still sat. "So, how does it feel to have them back?"

"It's good. Maybe it's not the way I planned, but I'm glad they're here. I'm glad Lindsey is here. She's going to have a rough road ahead of her."

"You have to give Jana some credit for bringing her back."

"Do I?"

"She risked a lot. For all she knew, you'd have the cops here waiting to arrest her."

"That's true."

"What do you plan on doing?"

"I'm going to take it one day at a time, and make sure Lindsey gets the care she needs."

Jackson shot him a look, shaking his head. "Yeah, that's a given. I mean what are you going to do about the ex-wife?"

"Get along with her for the sake of our daughter."

Jackson stood and glanced down at Blake, not smiling. "I hate to say this, since you're supposed to be older and wiser, but I think you've lost it if you think you're going to have an amicable but distant relationship with Jana."

"That's the only relationship I want with her."

"Right." Jackson pulled truck keys out of his pocket. "I'm heading home. I promised Maddie that I'd put something on the grill."

"I think I'll crash out here tonight."

"You can come over to my place for burgers. I think the folks have a dinner in Grove, some charity thing."

Blake pushed himself to his feet. The two of them started toward the door. "I need to spend time with Teddy. I think I'll pick him up and take him to the Mad Cow."

The Mad Cow was the local diner, the only diner, in Dawson. The owner, Vera, made the best coconut cream pie. Blake could use a piece of that pie right about now.

"Right. Teddy. How will you fit him into your life, now that Lindsey is back?" Jackson asked.

"I think she'll understand. He's five, and I can't walk out on him."

"True." Jackson adjusted his hat and slipped on a pair of sunglasses. "Have you talked to our little brother lately?"

Blake didn't have to ask. He knew Jackson meant Dylan.

"A few days ago. I told him I'd help them with the guardianship papers."

"Do you really think he should do this?"

Blake didn't have a clue what other people

should do with their lives. He was barely figuring out his own.

"He's determined, and he feels like he's the only one who can take Katrina's kids, should the worst happen."

"Well, let's pray the worst doesn't." Jackson sighed. "Are you going back to the office anytime soon?"

"I went for a few hours the other day. Most of what I'm working on I can do from here." Work was the last thing he wanted to think about right now.

"I'd offer to help, but since I'm not the family lawyer I doubt I'd do more than mess things up."

Blake laughed at that. "I'd like to send you into court for me."

"I'll leave the arguing up to you." Jackson climbed in his truck. "I know you're the guy used to making the hard decisions. Take your time on this one."

"On what?"

"On Jana. The jury is still out, Blake. I don't think I'd be too quick to find her guilty."

"Thanks for putting it in terms I can understand."

Jackson laughed an easy laugh. "I do try to help. Later, big brother."

Blake watched the truck ease down the drive

and then he headed for the house—the big, brick Georgian that he'd been raised in, he and eleven other Cooper kids, plus a few foster children. His parents knew how to fill a house with kids and with love.

They'd always said love didn't run out. There was enough to go around. He thought they'd used the same lecture about forgiveness. Over the years he'd convinced himself he'd forgiven Jana. Now, with her back and living in his house, he wasn't so sure.

Maybe forgiving Jana was something he'd have to work on. In the past few days there were other feelings cropping up he thought he'd let go of years ago. Those feelings made him a little more edgy.

When he got to the house he called Lisa, Teddy's mom and asked if Teddy could join him for dinner. He arranged to pick up the little boy in an hour. That gave him time to look for some paperwork in the office.

As he pushed through papers on the desk, he remembered something. He opened the filing cabinet.

Inside he found the manila envelope and poured the contents on the desk. Memories caught in snapshots of a marriage that had ended too soon. His baby girl smiled up at him, her face round and healthy, her eyes bright with laughter. She'd always been laughing. A few of the pictures were of Jana.

There were pictures of her before Lindsey. Jana with blond hair and laughing blue eyes. There was also their wedding photograph that used to hang in the living room. His heart shifted, forcing him to remember how much he'd loved her. He picked up a few pictures of Jana and Lindsey, lifting them close to study. The air hung heavy in the room, waiting for the air conditioner to kick on. He reached to turn on the lamp, needing to see more clearly.

There was something in those pictures of Jana that he hadn't noticed before.

Sadness.

But why? What had happened to her in those few short years that had changed her from that smiling young woman he'd fallen in love with to the woman with the haunted blue eyes who had left him.

And why hadn't he noticed then? Had he been too young, too happy, so her unhappiness took him by surprise when she tried to tell him? He'd brushed it off, ignored her quiet plea for help.

He didn't want to let her off the hook that easily. She'd taken their daughter and left the country. His life had been on hold for ten years. He hadn't tried to move on and find someone else. He'd spent ten years searching for Lindsey and being angry with Jana.

He slid the pictures back in the envelope. A letter had gotten mixed in with them. He picked it up, recognizing the return address as that of the divorce lawyer he'd used when Jana left. All of those years ago he'd signed for the letter and then tossed it in a box without opening it. He hadn't wanted to acknowledge the finality of the divorce. Even now he didn't want to read it. He shoved it in his pocket and instead of returning the manila envelope of photographs to the cabinet, he carried them with him from the room. Lindsey would like to see the pictures, he was sure.

His stomach rumbled, reminding him of a strong need for Vera's coconut cream pie. He also remembered Teddy. The little boy would be waiting for him on the front steps of his house, the way he always did when Blake was coming to pick him up.

Jana stepped out of the car at the Mad Cow. It hadn't changed at all. Same block building painted with black-and-white splotches like a Holstein cow. Same parking lot filled with a variety of cars and trucks. It was Friday and the special was cashew chicken.

"This is a restaurant?" Lindsey stepped next

to her, a little pale and hazel eyes big as she looked around.

"This is it." Jana's legs shook a little at the thought of going inside. People might recognize her. They might say something.

Eventually she had to face it. She was going to be here a long, long time. Lindsey's hand slipped into hers. Did Lindsey recognize that her mother might not be at her most confident?

"I'm hungry." Lindsey said it with conviction. "So, are we going in?"

"We're going in."

They walked across the gravel parking lot, holding hands. For a moment they were mother and daughter the way they had been a year ago. Before their world had started to fall apart. Before Jana had been forced to face her past and drag her daughter with her.

Because the past had been their only hope. This town, Blake, the Coopers. This was their future.

The cowbell hanging over the door clanged, announcing their arrival. The restaurant was crowded. People watched them as they walked into the diner, a few whispered, most went back to their meals. Jana scanned the dining area looking for an empty table. She hadn't counted on this, on the Mad Cow being so busy they couldn't get a table.

A waitress headed their way. She was tall and had long blondish-brown hair that was held back in a ponytail. Jana didn't know her. And from her smile, it was obvious she didn't know who Jana was.

"Just a minute and we'll get you ladies a table," she offered with a smile. Her name tag said Breezy.

Jana smiled and started to respond, but someone in the far corner called out to Breezy, telling her that Jana could join them. Lindsey was already heading toward the table filled with Coopers. Blake's sister Sophie, her husband, Keeton West, and their little girl, Lucy.

"I guess we'll sit with Sophie." Jana smiled up at Breezy.

"Sounds like a perfect plan. I was being optimistic thinking we could get you a table anytime soon." Breezy grabbed menus and followed her to the table.

Lindsey was already sitting next to the baby, Lucy. That left Jana sitting next to Keeton and across from Sophie.

"Thank you for letting us sit with you." Jana took the menu from Breezy and smiled at Sophie. "It's so busy."

"Always. Vera's the best cook around and the only restaurant in town."

"I hadn't really thought about it when we left the house."

Sophie moved her glass for Breezy to refill her water. "Is everything okay at Blake's? Do you need anything?"

"We're getting settled, and your mom left us plenty of food."

Sophie smiled at that. "Mom thinks of everything. And I'm glad she has you to focus on for a while. I'm due at the end of July and she's been hovering over me like a helicopter."

Jana didn't know what to say. Her parents had been older, adopting her when they were both nearly fifty. She'd lost them both before she graduated from college. In the past week Angie Cooper had been a blessing to Jana and Lindsey. She'd been there for them every step of the way.

She only wished she'd known years ago that she could talk to her mother-in-law. Angie would have understood the depression. She could have helped.

Water under the bridge, of course. Jana had to stop looking back or she'd get stuck in the mistakes of the past.

"I didn't mean to sound as if I'm complaining." Sophie's hand covered Jana's. "I'm so fortunate, and Mom is always there for us. She's so glad you're back."

"So am I." The words came out easily. "And I'm so glad Lindsey will have your family around her. She needs aunts, uncles and cousins."

Keeton laughed, "She'll have plenty. More than she can handle."

The cowbells clanged again. Sophie's eyes widened, so Jana shifted to see who had walked through the door. Of course it was Blake. He stepped inside, taking off his black cowboy hat as he did. And he wasn't alone. The little boy next to him wore a matching miniature cowboy hat. Jana swallowed, waiting, knowing she didn't have the right to ask for explanations.

When Blake spotted her, his smile dissolved. He glanced past her to their daughter.

Lindsey stood, nearly knocking over her chair. She didn't seem at all upset by the presence of the child at Blake's side. Instead she smiled big. "Daddy."

It came so easily. Her smile. Her love for him. His love for her. Jana watched as he crossed the room to their daughter's side. He wrapped her in a hug, the little boy, blond with big green eyes watched them together. Blake borrowed chairs from a table next to theirs. One for him and one for the child.

"I didn't expect to see you out tonight. I could

have given you a ride." He smiled at Lindsey, but his statement was directed at Jana.

The buzz of conversation in the restaurant quieted as people around them tried to listen in. Jana reached for her coffee, needing something to occupy hands that trembled. In time people would get tired of talking about them, about her. There would be new gossip. That's how it worked in a small town. She knew that.

Of course, she'd been giving them something to talk about for a long time.

"It was a last-minute decision." She sipped her coffee, not really tasting it.

Breezy reappeared with another menu, a child's menu and crayons. She put the paper and the crayons in front of the little boy, who didn't seem at all bothered by the group of people around him.

"What will we have tonight, Blake?" Breezy went around the table taking orders. When she got to Teddy, she ruffled his hair. "And my friend, Teddy?"

"I'm having chicken strips and fries, but I need some for my mom and sister, too." The boy, Teddy, picked up crayons and started to color the dinosaur picture on the menu.

Breezy looked at Blake, her pen poised above the order pad. He nodded. "Make sure we have two orders of chicken strips to go when we leave."

"Got it." She squatted in front of Teddy. "And Vera said kids' meals get sundaes tonight, if you eat most of your food."

"Most?" He grinned at her, a big smile that lit up his little face. Jana's heart took a dive, because she could see that a kid like Teddy would be easy to get attached to.

"Yes." Breezy stood, patted his head again and was off to place their order and refill drinks.

"How are you feeling?" Sophie asked her brother after the waitress left.

"Almost as good as new." He smiled as he said it, winking at Lindsey who grinned.

Jana listened, waiting for someone to mention the little boy and his place in her ex-husband's life. Why in the world should she be jealous? She'd left. Blake still had a life here. He had family. He had this little boy named Teddy.

"I went out and saw my pony after you left." Lindsey broke into the conversation, her smile huge. "He's tiny."

"Yes, he is." Blake leaned toward her. "But he's still strong. He pulls a cart."

"Do you think…?"

"No!" Jana hadn't meant to blurt it out. She bit down on her lip and shrugged when all eyes turned in her direction. "I'm sorry. You can't ride, Lindsey. You'll have to be careful."

Lindsey looked away. "I won't be able to do anything."

"That isn't true. We'll find things you can do. For now, though, we want you healthy." Blake used a dad tone of voice that sounded as if he'd been talking to his daughter her whole life.

A fresh pang of guilt washed over Jana. Lindsey could have had a dad who would have taught her things, laughed with her. Jana's own father had been a distracted businessman who never had the time or patience for a child.

Blake smiled at Jana. A smile that said they were on the same side.

Jana relaxed and thought of an option. "Maybe the wagon. You might be able to ride in it, after the doctors give their okay."

Lindsey brightened a little. "That would be good. And I can go to the rodeo. There's one coming up."

Their food arrived. Sophie and her family finished up their meal and stood, saying goodbye and hugging Lindsey before they gathered everything that went along with a toddler. Keeton touched her shoulder as they started to walk away.

"Let us know if you need anything."

She nodded and smiled at him.

After Sophie's family left, silence hung over the table. Jana tried to see them from the eyes of the people at other tables. A father. A daughter. A mom. But they weren't a family. They were fractured, broken.

The little boy, Teddy, looked up, a crayon poised in his hand. He looked at Lindsey. "Blake said you got one of his kidneys and that's why he's been gone."

Lindsey blinked a few times and then smiled. "Yeah, he gave me one of his."

"How did he give it to you?"

"Well…" Lindsey looked at Blake.

"We'll talk about that some other time, Teddy. Tell Lindsey what we're going to do next week," Blake encouraged with a smile.

Teddy's face lit up. "Go fishin'."

"Sounds like fun." Lindsey wasn't quite smiling. She looked at her dad.

"We can all go." Blake offered, including Jana. "Teddy has an older sister. Sissy is seven. She'd probably love to go with us."

Jana didn't know what to say. She nodded slowly, accepting the offer.

"Jana, are you okay?"

She nodded, smiling at her daughter. "I'm good. Just…" What did she say? She looked at Teddy, looked at Blake, and his eyes widened. He smiled.

"Teddy and I hang out together. He goes to Dawson Community Church and we're buddies."

Jana didn't know how to respond to this information. Before she could think of something to say, Vera and Breezy joined them, carrying sundaes. Vera hadn't changed at all. Jana had always liked the owner of the Mad Cow Café. Her dark hair might be pulled back in a severe bun, but the warmth in her eyes and the big smile on her face made it clear that she cared.

"Welcome home, Jana and Lindsey." Vera placed sundaes in front of each of them. "And this is for Teddy because he ate his dinner and for Blake because he gave the most important gift to his daughter."

Vera hugged Blake tight, and he turned a little red. "Thanks, Vera."

"You're welcome." She smiled at the four of them sitting at the table. "I love happy endings."

Jana thought one of them should say something, should let Vera know that this wasn't a happy ending. Not the way she meant. Instead Blake smiled and reached for his daughter's hand, and Jana thought maybe that was all the happy ending they needed.

When they were alone again, Blake picked up the manila envelope he'd placed on the table when he first arrived. He handed it to Lindsey.

"I thought you might like this. And there are other photographs. I'll try to find them. Maybe your mom has already shared some with you?"

Jana shook her head when Lindsey looked at her expectantly. "I have pictures in a box in London. I kept them there, along with a letter and of course my lawyer there had your contact information, Blake."

"I see."

It went without saying. She'd made arrangements in case something happened to her.

Lindsey had already opened the envelope. She was sifting through pictures, commenting and asking questions. Blake answered, bending close, their two dark heads so similar. As he talked to their daughter he pulled another envelope from his pocket and handed it to Jana.

"You might want a copy of this."

She took the envelope, noticing the name and address of a Tulsa law firm. The postmark was six months after she left. She knew that it would be their divorce papers. And it had never been opened. Why hadn't he opened it? She shoved the envelope in her purse.

She pretended it didn't matter. Across from her, Lindsey was sifting through photographs of a life that had ended years ago. She asked Blake questions and then showed the pictures to Teddy, who had moved to sit next to her.

The little boy laughed, looking up at Blake and then Lindsey.

The restaurant was starting to empty. Jana glanced at her watch as Lindsey studied picture after picture and Blake told her stories about the life she lived here.

"We should probably go so Vera can close," Jana finally suggested, smiling at the very sleepy-looking boy sitting next to Blake.

Blake looked around them. "You're right. Breezy deserves a good tip. We tied her table up all night. And Teddy is just about done in."

Teddy looked up. "I'm not tired."

"Of course you aren't. But I told your mom I'd have you home early."

Blake paid and walked them out to their car. It was a strange moment, standing in the parking lot with dusk settling over the small farm town of Dawson. The sky was hazy, and in the distance she heard the whistle of a train.

She'd lived in so many places since she'd left. Now that she was back, Dawson suddenly felt like the home she'd been looking for rather than the place she had run from.

Next to her Blake had settled his hat back on his head. He winked at Lindsey as he pulled keys out of his pocket.

"I'll see you Sunday at church?" He stared

her down, because of course he didn't believe she'd be there.

"We'll be there." She leaned to hug Teddy. "See you when we go fishing."

Teddy nodded and climbed in the open door of the truck. Blake stood there a little longer.

"Good night." Jana opened her car door.

Blake hugged their daughter, touched Jana's arm in a parting farewell and climbed in his truck. This was their new normal—two strangers raising a daughter together.

Chapter Six

Sunday morning, as she walked up the steps of Dawson Community Church, Jana had a strange sense of coming home. Of course she held Lindsey's hand a little tighter than her daughter would have liked. And she did imagine that everyone was talking about her. But it hadn't felt like this before. Years ago she'd made the effort each Sunday to attend church with Blake. But she had always felt out of place, like a stranger in a strange land. She hadn't understood the language, the devotion. She hadn't seen a need.

She'd felt like a captive back then. And she had been, she just hadn't realized it. She'd been captive to mistakes she had made, to the past, to fear.

Today she walked through the church free from all of that baggage. She needed to remember that. She had made mistakes but she was forgiven.

Blake's grandmother, Myrna Cooper, hurried forward to grab her hand. "I was a little worried you wouldn't come today. And we sure want you to join us for lunch at Cooper Creek."

"Thank you, I…"

Though Jana was unsure, there was no way that Lindsey wasn't going to Cooper Creek for lunch. Myrna's hand squeezed Jana's and she gave her a pleading look.

"Of course we'll be there."

Suddenly little Teddy stormed down the aisle of the church toward them as if they weren't strangers he'd met only once. Several people turned to watch. A few smiled. Teddy had hold of his sister's hand and he was grinning big.

"I lost a tooth," he informed them.

"You certainly did." Jana leaned to look at the open space in his mouth. "When?"

"I pulled it last night." He opened his mouth to show Lindsey. She grimaced and looked a little green. He didn't notice. "Can I sit with you?"

"I think you can." Lindsey allowed the little boy to lead her toward the front of the church, to pews that were already filling up with Coopers.

"It'll just hurt this first time." Granny Myrna patted Jana's arm. "People will stare. They'll talk a little. You'll hurt a little. And next time it will be as if you never left."

"Thank you, Myrna."

"I prefer Gran, or Granny Myrna." Myrna Cooper nodded to the empty spaces in one of the pews. "You can sit by me. I'm not sure where that grandson of mine is."

Jana had wondered the same thing. As she sat and the music started, she kept glancing back, wondering if Blake would make it to church. Maybe he wanted to avoid this. The first Sunday when they would have made awkward eye contact and tried to find the right things to say to each other.

For Jana, being here meant remembering the day she and Blake had stood with the pastor, holding their infant daughter and praying that they would be the parents God wanted them to be.

She hadn't been until recently. Now she was doing what she'd promised so long ago. God had remembered her promise, and He had brought her to this place where she could keep it.

She had also stood under an arch of white roses and promised to love Blake, to remain true to him, to love him in sickness and in health.

A little boy crawled into her lap, not caring that she'd taken a short trip into the past. He didn't seem to care what she'd done before.

He curled his arms around her neck and held tight, his eyes sleepy.

She swallowed past the tightness in her throat as he placed his head on her shoulder.

And Blake didn't walk through the doors of the church to sit with them.

Blake spent the morning watching over a mare in foal, knowing it wouldn't be an easy birth. And he'd been right. Her pacing and stomping had led to a long and difficult birth that ended with a pretty filly the color of her sire. The color he'd been hoping for. He'd wanted the mouse-colored dun stallion, but the best he could do was get a foal from him.

On the way to his folks' for lunch, he got a call from his mom, reminding him that Jana and Lindsey were joining them. She hoped he didn't mind.

He told her he didn't. When he hung up he remembered the conversation with the psychiatrist at the hospital when she asked him about his feelings for his ex-wife. After Jana took Lindsey, there had been people who thought maybe he needed counseling. He could admit he'd been half-crazed the first year. The next nine, he'd learned to control his emotions, not letting it get to him, even when it felt like everything he did, every breath he took, was about the daughter he couldn't find.

How did it feel to have them back in his life? To know they had returned only because there had been no other options for saving Lindsey? He had given the psychiatrist a simple answer. He would do whatever it took to save his daughter. To keep her in his life again.

But what about Jana? She would be in his life, too. How did he feel about that?

He gripped the steering wheel of the truck a little tighter and let out a long breath. Jana was part of the package. He could have her in his life and not throttle her. He knew that. But what bugged him most was the fact that when he thought of throttling her, he could only picture holding her close, and burying his face in her hair.

It would be only too easy to forget what she'd done.

So it wasn't good that he pulled up to the house to see her leaning in the backseat of her car, all golden tanned legs and high-heeled shoes. He got out of his truck as she backed out of the car holding a dish. Her blond hair was swept back from her face. The dress she wore was soft peach and made her look innocent and easy to hold.

"I forgot my pie," she said by way of explanation. "I had to run home and get it."

"Anything I can carry for you?" His mom had raised him to be a gentleman.

"No, I have it." She started to walk away. He stepped next to her.

"Where's Lindsey?"

She kept walking, the breeze blowing tendrils of hair across her face. He took the pie from her, and she looked up at him.

"She's inside with Lucky's children and Jackson's daughter. I'm still trying to come to terms with Jackson married with children."

"People change."

She stopped. He looked back and saw that her blue eyes shimmered with moisture. He wanted to swear, but he didn't. Instead he waited.

"People do change, Blake." Her words were as soft as the spring breeze. "*I've* changed. I know you say you've forgiven me, but I also know that you're still angry. I can't give you back the ten years I took. I can only give you today and the future."

"I know."

"I'm tired of trying to convince you that you can trust me."

"Stop trying."

"That's easy enough." She glanced away from him. A few tears trickled down her cheeks. "I'm so tired, Blake. I've been tired for so long. I've worried about Lindsey. I've worried about coming back. Now I worry about her future health. I don't have the energy to worry about you, too."

He closed the distance between them and an image of holding her close flashed through his mind. The image was easy to handle. The real thing was a whole different matter. If he held her in his arms, and it still felt like the most perfect fit in the world, then what?

"Jana, you're not alone. You did the right thing, coming back here."

She nodded and swept a hand across her cheek. He held on to the pie, because it gave his hands a reason not to touch her.

"Thank you for that, Blake. It's been easier, having you and your family for support."

They should go inside. She was looking up at him the way she'd done so many times in their marriage. She had a way of looking lost and hopeful at the same time. She was a woman who had come to the States to study the history of the American West, and to trace one of her ancestors, her great-great-grandfather, who had moved to America, leaving behind his wife and children in England. He'd wanted to find gold and come home wealthy.

He had sent home money but had died of

some fever. Blake couldn't believe he remembered that story.

Worse, why would this be the moment it came to mind? Maybe because he was looking into her eyes and seeing that college coed who had taken a chunk out of his heart just four short years later.

"We should go inside." He glanced down at the pie in his hands. "Chocolate?"

"Your favorite." She still didn't move. "I brought Teddy with me. I hope you don't mind. His sister went home with another family, and his mother didn't feel well. Your mom called to make sure it was okay if we brought him with us."

He sighed and shook his head. There were things in life that took a man by surprise. Jana had always been one. Falling in love with her. Coming home to an empty house. And this moment. She had always taken him by surprise.

"I'm glad you brought him."

They entered the house together. The living room was empty. He could hear everyone gathered in the kitchen and the formal dining room. From the family room he heard the voices of kids playing. He caught Lindsey's voice in the mix. Suddenly it all felt right. As if the lost years had never happened.

He and Jana were walking through the house.

Their daughter was playing with her cousins. There was no heartache, no loss, no sick child to worry over. It was a momentary lapse on his part, but he went with it because it had been so long since everything felt right.

Lindsey must have heard them. She came running out of the family room into the dining room. Her dark hair was in a ponytail. Her cheeks were pink. Her hazel eyes flashed with excitement.

He wanted to pick her up and throw her in the air, but she wasn't two years old anymore. Instead he hugged her tight.

"I was afraid you weren't going to come." She spoke into his shirt as he held her close, then she struggled to get free. "Don't squeeze me to death."

"Sorry, I'm making up for lost hugs."

"You can't make up for them—they're like sleep." She shook her head as if that made perfect sense. "You don't make up for them. You just go back to normal."

"From the mouths of babes." Granny Myrna walked into the room in time to hear his daughter's bit of wisdom. Granny Myrna looked overjoyed, and behind her was the reason. Her fiancé, Winston McDaniels.

Lindsey gave Blake a narrow-eyed look. "Where were you, anyway?"

"I had to help a mare deliver her first foal."

Lindsey's smile returned. "Can I see it?"

"Maybe later."

"Is it a girl or a boy?"

"It's a girl." He put an arm around her shoulder. "Let's go see if lunch is almost ready. I'm starving."

"Me, too!" She gave her mother a questioning look, and Jana nodded. Lindsey walked with him to the kitchen, where it smelled as if the best restaurant in Oklahoma had descended into the family kitchen.

"What's for lunch?" He set the pie on the counter and walked up behind his mom to give her a quick hug.

"Beef tenderloin. I had your dad put it on the smoker."

"Tenderloin? What's the occasion?"

"You have to ask?" she said with a smile.

No, he didn't have to ask. A special meal for his daughter. He looked around the room and Lindsey had disappeared. Jana was standing there though, looking a little lost.

"Is there something I can do to help?" he asked his mom as he reached for a slice of bread, knowing she wouldn't let him. She slapped his hand away, the way she always did. He looked down into eyes that were so familiar, but aging. When had that happened? Then again, he'd recently noticed some silver in his hair and lines at the corners of his eyes.

"Spend time with your daughter." His mom squeezed his arm and then moved away to stir something on the stove.

He left the kitchen and found Lindsey back in the family room. She and Jade were looking at photo albums with Teddy curled up between them. Jade was fifteen now, and she'd grown into a great kid. She might not be Jackson's flesh and blood, but Blake didn't think any kid could be more like Jackson than Jade. She had his hair, his eyes; she even acted like him. Blake figured that might be a problem in a few years.

Lindsey looked up and smiled at him. "We're looking at family pictures. Christmas is a big deal around here."

He sat down next to her. "Yes, it is. What part do you like the best."

She pointed to a picture of the living nativity. "I want to have a part."

"I'm sure you will."

She and Jade talked. One sounding like the Oklahoma kid she was, the other with an accent that came from time spent in Europe and Africa.

A flash out of the corner of his eye caught his attention. Jana stood in the doorway watching, and then silently walked away, giving them time alone. He would thank her for that later. It couldn't be easy, letting go.

His mind suddenly raced to an idea that didn't sit too well with him. What if her plan was to leave Lindsey? What if she packed up and left again?

What unsettled him more was the idea of her being gone again. It shouldn't, he decided. He had his daughter back, and that had been his goal all along. He'd been searching the world for Lindsey, not Jana.

Maybe the first six months after Jana left he'd thought he could find her and they could work things out. But when she didn't call, didn't write, he gave up hope of reconciliation and focused on finding Lindsey. He had known that somewhere out there a little girl had to be missing him. If Jana had missed him, she could have called.

Jana walked into the living room, needing time alone. Space. She'd never been good with crowds, at the feeling of being suffocated by Coopers. There were so many of them. They talked loud, they laughed loud and they lived loud. She'd grown up in a quiet home, just herself and her parents. They had never raised their voices. Ever.

She'd never learned to be strong. Strength

was something she'd found after learning of Lindsey's kidney failure. Strength was still coming to her. And faith. In the beginning stages of her marriage, it had bothered her when she learned that the Coopers put so much into something her parents had seen as archaic, just an old tradition.

Now she understood faith. She understood pleading for peace and finding it in an overwhelming way. She now understood the strength that came from knowing there was a God and He had a plan.

It wasn't archaic; it was relevant. She was living proof. She had tried on her own to find peace, to forgive herself, to get through her daughter's illness. She'd been drowning until Lindsey begged her to go to church. Lindsey had found faith in a private school Jana had sent her to. A school she attended with the children of missionaries in Africa.

Jana took in a deep breath and focused on family portraits on the wall. She'd seen these same pictures years ago. As more grandchildren were born, as the children got older, pictures were added to the wall. Only Lindsey's progress had been frozen in time. There were pictures of Blake, but their wedding picture was gone. Left in its place were pictures of Lindsey as a baby, at one year of age and a picture of Lindsey at her second birthday sitting on her pony.

Their lives had stood still in time, stopped in Lindsey's second year. No one but Jana and a friend knew how difficult that year had been for her.

Jana swallowed a hard lump of regret. She felt someone walk up behind her. She turned and smiled at Myrna Cooper. Myrna touched her shoulder as she came to her side.

"Don't let regret swallow you up, Jana. We all make mistakes."

"Not this big, we don't."

"Oh, honey, you can't undo the past. You can only make the future better. Not just for Blake and Lindsey, but for yourself, too."

Jana nodded, because she didn't trust herself to speak. The kind words, the kind expressions, would be her undoing. If she opened her mouth to answer she would probably cry. Myrna seemed to understand. Instead of pushing the conversation, she put names to faces, catching Jana up on new additions to the family and changes that had taken place.

"I have your wedding ring." Myrna's words came at the end of the conversation.

"I'm sorry?"

"You left your wedding ring on the table. Blake was beside himself when he got home and you were gone. He picked up the ring and came over here. When he left to go back home he tossed the ring on the counter. I thought it best if I held it for safekeeping."

"Myrna, I…" Jana didn't know what to say, how to respond.

"When the time is right, you'll know what to do."

"I'm not sure what you mean."

Myrna smiled at that. "You young people are so funny to an old bird like myself. You think you make your own destiny? You think that all of this happens by accident? I have one important bit of advice for you. Don't run. Stay and see things through."

"I'm not leaving again."

"But there will be times that you're tempted. It isn't as if this is going to be easy, living here, being thrown back into the life of the man you left."

"No, it won't be easy."

"Remember that you're not alone. You have people you can talk to. Including me."

"Thank you, Myrna. I'll remember."

Myrna raised a bejeweled hand. "That's Granny Myrna to you. Don't let this group get to you. Especially Mia. She isn't your biggest fan. Heather is running a close second in anger. They love their older brother."

"I know I don't have a fan club."

Myrna gave her a swift hug. "But you have friends. Now, I think we should go help set the table."

She walked to the kitchen with Myrna. They put pitchers of water and sweet tea on the table and filled glasses while Heather and Elizabeth, Travis Cooper's wife, set the table.

And then she found herself seated next to Mia. Blake sat across from her, and Lindsey had picked a seat at the second table so she could sit with Jade. That left Jana stranded in what felt like enemy territory.

"Bought a plane ticket yet?" Mia scooped asparagus onto her plate and passed the serving dish to Jana.

"No, actually, I haven't."

Mia smiled and took a few new potatoes before passing the bowl. "That's good. We all love having Lindsey back. Blake hasn't been this happy in, oh, ten years."

"I'm sorry, Mia."

Mia started to say something else, but Blake shot her a look that shut her up quick.

Blake turned his attention to Teddy, who had taken the seat next to his. Jana listened as the two discussed fishing and riding horses. They talked about Teddy's mom, because Teddy said she slept a lot.

Jana's heart got a little more tangled up as she listened to the little boy talk about the messy house, the cold soup for meals and a mom who could barely crawl out of bed. It all sounded so familiar.

Blake glanced her way, not smiling. Their gazes connected, and she knew she had to tell him what her life had been like before she left Oklahoma.

After the meal, Jana helped clear the table. Around her, conversations drifted; Sophie laughed at something Madeline said. Heather managed to smile and tell Jana about her new house. She was moving back to Dawson from Grove. Jana shared that she thought when the time was right she would find a house in Dawson and maybe a job. It was a simple conversation but it was a start.

When everything was cleaned up, Jana escaped out the patio door. Blake had disappeared into the family room with Teddy. Lindsey had followed Jade somewhere. Jana needed to breathe deep and clear her head. A few minutes later the door opened and Blake walked out. He stretched and then touched his side, grimacing.

"Are you okay?" Jana looked away from him to study the way the breeze caused the water in the pool to ripple across the surface.

"I'm obviously better than you are." Blake

walked up next to her. "I've talked to Mia. She'll back off."

"She loves her brother and I hurt him. I think she has a right to be angry."

"She takes it too far." Blake stood next to her, his arm brushing hers.

"I really need to go, Blake. It was kind of your family to include me today, but maybe it would be better if the family dinners don't include the ex-wife who kidnapped your daughter."

"That isn't what they think of you."

"I think a few of them do. What about you?"

He looked down at her, studying her face, his hazel eyes more blue today, with hints of green and gray. "I don't know what I think anymore."

"It probably doesn't help that you can't turn around without me being in what used to be your space."

"I'm working through that." He smiled a little, and in that smile she saw the old Blake. The shadows lifted from his eyes, from his expression. "I can bring Lindsey home after I take Teddy home."

Teddy. "Blake, his mother. It sounds as if she needs help."

He cocked his head a little to the side and stared at her for a long minute. "Why do you think that?

"Because I…" She closed her eyes, then spoke. "I'm familiar with the symptoms of depression."

He took her by the arm and they started walking. "This sounds like a conversation we should have had a long time ago."

They stopped after they'd walked a distance from the house. A big oak tree gave them shade and a light breeze blew.

"Your turn," Blake said, studying her face with an intensity that made her want to take back what she had said.

"There's so much to say, Blake. I'm not sure if this is the time."

"It seems like the time to me."

"Okay. But it won't be easy."

He shrugged powerful shoulders and he didn't smile. She knew it had to be said, but it hurt, just thinking about it hurt.

"Blake, I had a miscarriage."

"What? When?" The word shot out, cold and hard.

She closed her eyes, unable to look at the pain in his. "Six months before I left. I didn't know how to tell you. I already felt like a failure, a fraud, and the miscarriage toppled my emotions. I didn't realize it at the time, but I think I developed postpartum depression with

Lindsey, and the miscarriage threw me into a tailspin that I didn't see coming."

For a long time he didn't say anything. His hand had been on her arm, but it dropped and he walked away. She watched him gather himself. His hand rubbed the back of his neck, and he stared out at the field. She gave him a minute and then she walked up behind him.

"I made one bad choice after another." She wanted to touch his hand, hold it, but she didn't. She stood next to him, not touching him. "I know you might not be able to forgive me. I've had a hard time forgiving myself. But I thought you should know. Not because it's an excuse for what I did, but I just…"

"You could have told me."

She nodded, because her throat constricted, and she couldn't get the words out.

"I'm not even sure what to say to you, Jana. I would have done anything for you. I would have walked on hot coals to make things right for you."

"And I walked away." She sobbed on the words. "I know."

He looked down at her, his eyes a storm of emotion. "I'm not sure where to go from here."

"We focus on keeping our daughter healthy. And we take it one day at a time."

"I guess that's our only option."

She turned and he walked with her. "I should go. You'll bring Lindsey home?"

"Yeah. Do you have anything in the house?"

So that's how they were going to play it? They were going to walk away from the pain and pretend as if it hadn't happened. They were strangers with a daughter.

"No, I left my purse in the car."

Blake walked with her to the car. They stood there for several minutes, the breeze blowing around them, dust clouds kicking up across the field.

"I should go." She finally managed to find words to release her from the moment that seemed to have them both frozen.

"Yes." He reached to brush the hair from her face. "And, Jana, I'm sorry you thought you had to go through that alone."

She was, too. The softness in his voice brought tears that she blinked away. And then he leaned in, taking her by surprise.

When his mouth touched hers, she forgot to breathe. He brushed his lips across hers, soft, tentative, before fully claiming her, his hands cupping her cheeks.

He ended the kiss, but he held her close, and she inhaled the familiar outdoors, leather and spice scent that was all his. It felt like coming home. But she knew it wouldn't last. He could comfort her for a moment. Maybe they were comforting each other, ten years too late.

But any moment he would remember what she'd done, and his anger would return. For that reason she pulled back. And she immediately saw it in his eyes. Regret.

"I shouldn't have done that." Blake inhaled a deep, shaky breath. "Jana, I don't want to go back to that place where I spend years feeling like I have a big hole in my life."

"I know." She knew he wouldn't believe it if she told him she'd had a matching wound in her own life, the place in her heart that missed him.

He nodded, and she noticed his hand trembled as he brushed his palm across his cheek. "I'll bring Lindsey home later."

She slid behind the wheel of the car, thankful for the support because her legs had gone suddenly weak.

Somehow she managed a quiet "Thank you."

As she drove away, Blake stood in the driveway watching. She could see him in her rearview mirror, and there was something about that image that unsettled her.

She glanced back one last time, saw him wave then walk toward the house. The car kept going, putting more and more distance between them.

But this time she wasn't really leaving.

Chapter Seven

On Monday, Blake left work in the afternoon and headed for his place. He'd received a panicked call from Lindsey telling him the new foal looked sick. He asked her how she knew, and she admitted she'd been to the barn to pet her pony and give sugar cubes to the horses in the field. He'd told her to stay out of the stall and that he'd be there in thirty minutes.

He had checked the mare and filly late the previous night. The lights of the house had been off. He'd actually gone not just to check the foal but to talk to Jana. Because a kiss like the one they'd shared would be easy to misinterpret. He knew he was having a hard time putting the right label on that moment.

He pulled up to the house, but his gaze shifted to the corral where the mare grazed and the foal tried out new legs, prancing a little in the thick grass. Neither one of them seemed ill. He'd been played by a twelve-year-old. He grinned a little then swallowed the small grain of pride, because she'd have to learn that what she'd done was wrong.

As he got out of the truck Jana came out of the house. He reminded himself of the talk he'd been planning to have with her. There was nothing between them but a crazy past and a daughter.

Jana walked down off the porch, blond and delicate in a bright blue sundress. For years he'd brushed off the memories of what it had felt like to hold her. Now, because of yesterday, the memories were no longer images he could barely grasp. That moment of lost control meant he remembered that her skin was soft and she smelled like summer sunshine. And she tasted like honey.

He could pull himself out of those memories by remembering what she'd shared with him the previous day. A lost child, depression. After years of thinking one way about his disappearing wife, he now had to process this new information.

It was like trying to go to court without all of the evidence. That wasn't a good feeling in court or in life.

"I didn't expect you." She spoke softly with

that British accent that made her sound sweet, even when she was angry.

"Lindsey called to tell me the new foal was sick and I should come home as soon as possible."

Jana smiled a little but then hid it with a frown. He grinned, because he'd had the same reaction.

"I'm so sorry." She maintained a straight face. "I hope you weren't working on something important."

"I was just finishing up. And I can see the mare and foal are fine."

"I'll get your daughter for you. She's in her room."

"I'd appreciate that."

Jana paused on the steps. "Don't be too hard on her."

"I don't plan on it."

"No, I guess you don't."

"Tell her I'll be in the barn." In response, she nodded and headed for the house.

He headed for the barn. Might as well feed and take care of a few chores since he was there. He grinned again, because he knew the game Lindsey was playing. It reminded him of something his Granny Myrna would pull if she was in a matchmaking mood. But that didn't make it right. Lindsey had lied. He had to be the dad, and he was definitely out of practice.

He was checking the cattle when Lindsey showed up. He nodded in her direction and walked away from a heifer that had somehow managed to get cut. Probably an old barbed wire out in the field. He'd have to see if he could find it before some animal got tangled up good.

"You lied to get me out here?" he said to his daughter as they headed toward the barn.

She shrugged. She'd been sick, but that didn't mean she hadn't grown up along the way. He hadn't had time to prepare for this, for being a dad to a teen girl. There would be boys and cars, fights, everything that went along with raising a daughter. The thought of raising a girl in this day and age could bring down even the strongest of men.

Especially when his first inclination was to give her everything she wanted. Since he couldn't give her a whole family, couldn't give her two parents that were married and in love.

"I'm sorry." She walked up to the stall. The mare had come in through the open door, her foal next to her. Lindsey stood on tiptoe to watch the horse eat. He realized she was bare-foot.

"Where are your shoes?"

"In the house. She is pretty."

"Yes, she is. Why did you tell me the foal is sick?"

"Mom is making spaghetti for dinner. Her spaghetti is the best, and I thought maybe you could eat with us."

The mare raised her head from the bucket and grain dribbled from her mouth. The foal had moved in to nurse and was pushing against her side. What was he supposed to say?

Did the right words for this situation even exist?

"Linds, I know this is tough, but you have to understand, your mom and I are divorced. We're a family. You and I. You and your mom. But all three of us, we're…"

"But we're not really a family," she interrupted. "I know. I get it. But you don't understand that I've been looking for you for years."

He stopped her. "What do you mean, looking for me? I thought you didn't really know about us?"

"I knew I had a dad and if you were alive, I figured maybe you would write my mom. I always checked the mail, in case there was a letter. And I searched online. I dreamed about you. I wrote letters I couldn't send because I didn't know where you lived and I didn't know your name."

"Then how did you look for me?"

"I remembered you on the horse and one time, a long time ago, I heard Mom talking to someone, telling them about my dad. I knew my last name was Cooper. I just didn't know where you lived."

His heart broke in a million new pieces, and he pulled her close, holding her tight. He wasn't the only one who had missed out on years of being together, on moments they should have shared. School events, life events. They had both been missing each other.

"I'm here now." He kissed the top of her head and she wiggled from his arms, brushing away tears.

"I know."

"So let's make a deal. You don't have to come up with excuses to see me. You just have to call. If I'm busy with work, I'll tell you, and we'll make a time to be together." *Make time to be together*—even to him it sounded lame. "I'm not sure how this whole father-daughter thing works, Lindsey, but we'll figure it out. And you can help me."

"But I don't really know what a dad is supposed to do."

He smiled at her and there was only one answer. "They slay giants, Linds. That's what they do."

"Giants like kidney failure?" Her smile had faded and she looked away, her watery gaze focusing on the mare again.

"That was just a small giant. Dads are there to make sure boys you date act like gentleman, that broken hearts never happen and that flat tires get changed."

She grinned up at him. "I'm glad you're my dad."

"Me, too. And I'll always be here for you."

"I'm sorry for the call and for lying to you." She reached to pet the mare.

"I know."

It wouldn't be the last time they had a talk like this. Even though she shouldn't have made the call, he was glad she had, glad they were together and glad he could have these conversations with her. These were the discussions he'd thought he might never have.

Behind him, the door to the barn opened, letting in a shaft of late-afternoon sunlight that sent dust particles dancing on the beam of light. Jana stood in that light, hesitant, unsure, the golden light framing her silhouette.

"Everything okay out here?" She walked up to their daughter and put her arms around Lindsey, looking over her head at him.

"Yeah, everything is fine." He winked at Lindsey and then smiled at Jana, even though it wasn't easy. "I hear you make pretty decent spaghetti."

"So I've been told." She looked unsure as her eyes sought his. "Do you want to join us?"

"If you don't mind."

They walked to the house together, Jana a little off to the side, Lindsey holding his hand.

"Do you like French bread?" Lindsey asked as they walked up the steps of the house and through the front door.

"Yes, I do." He held the door open for his daughter and Jana.

"Mom makes the best." Lindsey smiled at her mom, obviously overlooking the tension between her parents.

Blake looked at his ex-wife. "You bake bread now?"

"And homemade spaghetti sauce," Lindsey added.

Pink crept into Jana's cheeks. "I've had a few years to learn to cook."

"Mom couldn't cook?" Lindsey had hold of his hand again and was leading him to the kitchen.

"No, I couldn't." Jana lifted the lid from a pot on the stove and stirred. "I had never cooked. It made for some interesting meals."

"Interesting?" Blake laughed an easy laugh that felt pretty good. "I remember something with sausage and chicken with vegetables in macaroni and cheese?"

Jana filled a second pot with water and put it on the stove, turning the burner to high. He watched, sitting at the island, his daughter next to him.

"I just knew that you liked pasta and meat. Your mom told me if I could fix pasta I'd make you happy. I had no idea how, so I bought macaroni and cheese, followed the directions and threw in some meat and peas, I think."

"Yes, the peas. I'd forgotten. I think you also put some boiled eggs in it."

"It wasn't horrible."

He smiled, remembering how she'd cried and he'd tried to eat the gunk on his plate. "It wasn't horrible."

And then they'd made up, and that hadn't been horrible. They'd eaten at the Mad Cow a lot after that. Or he'd cooked on the grill. They'd found ways to overcome her lack of culinary skills.

They did have good memories between them, he thought. He'd just chosen to forget them. He'd worked on forgetting the woman who had broken his heart. And now he didn't know her. She'd become someone else in the years since she'd left.

Maybe the woman she'd become was a woman he could admire.

Jana sliced the bread, trying to forget those early years when she'd always felt like a failure. She didn't want him to know that after she left she'd bought a cookbook with nothing but pasta recipes. She had taught herself to cook something other than chocolate pie, the one thing she'd known how to fix for him. Granny Myrna had taught her to make that pie.

"Jana?"

She looked up from the bread she was slicing. "I'm sorry. I got lost in thought."

"Do you need me to do anything?"

She shook her head, "No. I have everything ready. I'll cook the pasta and we'll be ready to eat. Lindsey, do you want to get the salad and dressing out of the fridge?"

Lindsey hopped down from the stool, flinching as she landed. Jana glanced from her daughter to Blake. Worry tightened in her chest, burning there as she watched her daughter.

"Lindsey, what's wrong?"

"I'm fine, Mom. It was just a twinge."

Blake was on his feet next to her. "Go sit down. I'll get the salad and set the table."

"Dad, I've got this."

Jana added the spaghetti pasta to the boiling water and stirred it to keep it from sticking. "Lindsey, sit down. A long day is a good reason to rest."

Lindsey huffed her dislike and went to the table, pulling out a chair and plopping down. Jana left the spaghetti to boil and she touched her wrist to her daughter's forehead.

"You feel warm to me."

Lindsey moved away, her eyes shimmering with unshed tears. "I'm fine. Please don't do this. Don't panic every time I cringe, or even feel a little sick. I'm not rejecting the kidney."

"Maybe not, but we have to be cautious."

"I know, but I don't want you to freak out every time something happens."

"I promise I'll try not to." Jana glanced toward the stove. Blake was stirring the spaghetti. "I'm going to finish cooking our dinner and then we'll take your temperature."

"Okay." Lindsey brushed away a tear. "But I'm fine."

Jana hoped she was fine. She wondered if the fear of kidney rejection would ever go away. Would they live each day, wondering if something would go wrong? Or would they learn to relax, to just trust God and accept the gift of second chances?

She took the long spoon from Blake and moved him out of the way. He didn't comment, but his arm slid around her waist and he gave her a quick hug, tugging her against his side just briefly before he walked away.

After he left her side she let a few tears fall, blinking to keep the storm of emotion at bay. How could she stay here, loving him and knowing he would never really let her back into his life?

She knew the answer. She stayed for her daughter. She would do anything for Lindsey, even stay here with Blake in her life but not really in her life.

A few minutes later they sat down to dinner together. Lindsey, Jana and Blake. Jana took the hand Blake offered and reached across the table for Lindsey's hand. Blake held their daughter's other hand. They bowed their heads and he asked a blessing on the food, on their lives and on their daughter's health. Jana closed her eyes tight, fighting the way she ached deep down inside.

Blake released her hand. She looked up and somehow managed a smile. She even managed to eat and to have conversation that seemed normal.

All the while her gaze kept straying to her daughter's pale face. Worry needled her, making her doubt everything.

"This is really good." Blake took a second

helping. When she looked at him, he grinned. "I mean it."

"You told me the macaroni and cheese gunk was good, too," she reminded.

"I didn't mean that."

Lindsey stirred the spaghetti around her plate. It was her favorite. Jana reminded her of that, and she shrugged.

"I think I'm going to go to bed," Lindsey finally said, standing up from the table with the barely touched plate of spaghetti.

Jana glanced at Blake and then back to her daughter. "Maybe we should call your brother Jesse or go to the emergency room."

"Mom, I'm fine. Remember, they said I'd be tired."

"I know, but…" Jana took a deep breath, told herself to relax, and somehow she smiled. "You're right. Get some sleep, and we'll leave early for Tulsa."

"Doctor's appointments, great." Lindsey kissed Jana's cheek and then rounded the table to hug her dad. "Are you going with us?"

"Of course I am. I have post-op checkups, too."

Jana started to stand but Lindsey stopped her. "Mom, I think I'm past being tucked in at night."

"Right, of course you are."

Jana got it. Her daughter was too old to be tucked in, but not too old to try to push her parents together.

"I'll help you do the dishes." Blake pushed himself to his feet and started gathering plates.

"You don't have to." Jana carried the plate of bread and their glasses to the sink. "I can do this later."

"I can help you now, and we'll be done twice as quick."

He'd always said that. They would do the dishes together each night and then they would sit on the front porch as the sun went down.

"I missed you." She said it softly, not sure if he wanted to hear or was ready to listen.

He didn't respond. He rinsed the last dish and stacked it in the drainer before looking at her, his hazel eyes dark, studying her face.

"I missed you, too." He leaned against the counter, his hands settled on her waist. "And that's the part that makes it hard to let you walk back into my life as if it never happened."

"I know and I understand." She stood on tiptoe and kissed his cheek. "I'm sorry."

He looked around the now-clean kitchen. "I have to go. We need to be on the road by seven tomorrow morning."

"We'll be ready. Do you want me to pick you up?"

He grinned at that, and she remembered how much she loved that smile of his. "No, I think I'll do the driving this time."

She walked him to the front door. He didn't kiss her goodbye. He didn't hug her. He did tell her to sleep well and not to worry.

A few minutes later he drove down the driveway and she was alone again. She prayed it wouldn't always be this way. Maybe it hadn't been her intention when she came home, to find a way to fix things with Blake. But everything had changed, and she knew she would do whatever she could to fix her marriage, to make them a family again.

Chapter Eight

Blake breathed a sigh of relief after Lindsey's appointment. She wasn't in rejection. The doctor had given them a list of symptoms to watch for, but he was convinced Lindsey was in the clear. What he didn't want was for her to get sick at this stage, so they needed to watch her and do their best to keep her healthy.

As they headed home from the hospital, Lindsey leaned over from the backseat of his truck, where she'd been listening to music on the MP3 player Mia bought her.

"Remember your promise." Lindsey flicked his shoulder. "We're taking Teddy fishing as soon as we get home."

"I haven't forgotten."

Jana glanced his way, her mouth a tight line of pretty obvious disapproval. "Should we?"

"Take Teddy fishing?" Blake asked, knowing she meant Lindsey.

"Should Lindsey go fishing?" Jana shot him the look normally reserved for a kid that had gotten into dessert and made a mess.

"Dr. Everton said she should take it easy and watch for signs of rejection but she should also do what she feels like doing. Within reason." The last was for his daughter. In case she got any ideas.

"Fishing isn't dangerous, and Teddy is looking forward to this." Lindsey turned her attention to her mom. "We can't let a little kid down."

Jana laughed at that. "Right, I'm just not sure if Teddy is the little kid you're worried about letting down."

She responded with mock teen hurt. "Of course I'm worried about Teddy. He's awesome."

"I talked to his mom last night, and she gave permission for him to spend the afternoon and evening with us. Sissy is at a friend's house." He glanced at Jana. "Is that okay with you, if we take him?"

Her face mirrored her confusion. "Blake, you don't have to ask my permission. You were spending time with Teddy before we came back to town, and I definitely wouldn't want you to stop just because we're here now."

"Jana, I'm asking because I thought you'd like to go with us." That might prove to be a mistake on his part, asking Jana to go with them, but it seemed right to have her along.

"Me?"

"Yeah, you." He glanced in the rearview mirror. Lindsey had settled back in her seat, but her eyes flicked from him to her mom and she had a pretty happy smile on her face. He'd give her anything, slay any giant, but he didn't know if he could give her what she wanted.

How did he tell his daughter not to get her hopes up when it came to her parents getting back together?

How did he not try to give her that?

"I'd like to go," Jana finally answered. "I can thaw out hamburgers to cook on the grill."

Blake eased through the city traffic. "Does that mean you don't think we'll catch fish?"

Her smile returned. "Oh, I didn't realize that you planned to catch fish."

Lindsey groaned. "Such a low blow. You know I always catch fish."

"Where have you fished?" Blake asked as they headed out of town. There were a lot of blank spaces in his daughter's life, things he didn't know and wanted to know.

"In Holland. Sometimes in the ocean but also in a river."

"Did you go to school there?"

She shook her head. "Mom homeschooled me in Holland. In Africa I went to a private school."

"Where did you like living the best?" He kept his attention on the road, but he glanced in the rearview mirror, and saw her eyes narrow as she looked at him. "What?"

"That's a silly question."

"Is it?"

"Yeah, because this is my favorite place to be."

They drove on in silence, but if a man's heart could burst at the seams, his was pretty close. Jana looked at him before focusing on the window. He saw her pain and knew it wasn't because Lindsey was happy. It was because their daughter had missed out.

When they reached Dawson, he drove through town, turning on a little side street that led to the tiny house where Teddy lived.

The little boy must have been watching for them, because the truck hadn't come to a complete stop and Teddy was out the door, a grin splitting his face. He was wearing shorts that were too big, a long-sleeved shirt, boots and a cowboy hat. He had a fishing pole that was barely three feet long.

Blake got out of the truck, and Lindsey ran

out her door to greet the little boy. Teddy hugged her first and then hugged Blake.

"I'm ready to go," he announced with another smile, this one showing the dimple in his left cheek.

"We need to tell your mom." Blake ruffled the blond hair and headed for the house. Teddy hurried to keep up.

"She's sleeping."

Blake stopped. Jana had gotten out of the truck, and she looked at him, then at Teddy.

"Let me knock on the door," she offered.

Teddy shook his head. "She doesn't want to be woke up. I tried, but she said to let her sleep and to catch lots of fish."

Jana obviously wasn't in the mood to listen. And Blake wasn't in the mood to stop her. He'd learned a long time ago that when a woman made up her mind about something, it was better to just let her go. And in this situation, he thought she might have a better idea how to handle things.

Teddy's hand slipped into his, but Blake's mind traveled eleven years into the past, remembering Jana sleeping a lot, forgetting to bathe the baby, forgetting lunch dates. He should have paid more attention.

"She's going to be mad," Teddy whispered as Jana knocked on the door.

"It will be okay, buddy. Jana just wants to make sure your mom isn't sick."

"She has a headache," Teddy informed him, sounding a lot older than a five-year-old should have to sound.

Jana didn't get an answer to her second or third knock so she went in, calling out to Teddy's mom. Blake waited with Teddy and a worried Lindsey. After a few minutes Jana returned. She shook her head.

"No luck?"

"I offered to take her to the doctor," Jana shared and then she quickly glanced at the little boy climbing in the truck with Lindsey.

Blake shut the door behind them. "What do you think we should do?"

"I'm not sure if we can do anything, Blake. She refuses to get help."

"I'll see if Wyatt and Rachel Johnson can talk to her. They might have better luck." The pastor and his wife knew how to reach people.

"She's worried about her kids." Jana's blue eyes were bright, and he could only think about hugging her, telling her he was sorry he hadn't noticed when she needed him.

He cleared his throat. "We'll make sure the kids are taken care of."

"I told her that." She smiled a little. He couldn't help himself. He leaned to kiss her. It was the briefest of gestures, but he could tell it took her by surprise.

It took him by surprise.

"We should go."

An hour later, they were in a boat on Grand Lake with the water lapping at the shore and water birds swooping overhead. Blake sat at the front, his foot on the trolling motor. Lindsey was baiting a hook for Teddy. He glanced over her head and made eye contact with Jana. She wasn't fishing. Instead she sat in a seat staring out at the water, a faraway look in her eyes.

She must have felt him watching because she turned to smile at him. The breeze picked up, blowing her hair across her face. Her hand came up to brush it back. If he could have, he would have asked what she was thinking and if she regretted being in Dawson. How did a person go from traveling the world to settling down in a small town in Oklahoma?

At that moment, Lindsey let out a screech and Teddy yelled even louder. His thoughts of Jana, the questions he wanted to ask, were replaced by the excitement unfolding in front of him.

"We've got one." Lindsey smiled big and thumped Teddy on the back. "Or Teddy does."

"Do you need help reeling it in?" Blake asked, leaning forward to watch.

Teddy shook his head and kept cranking,

the pole bending with the weight of the fish. Lindsey stood behind him, helping him hold the grown-up fishing pole they had traded his little one for. It took them both to bring in the bass on the end of Teddy's line.

"Good job." Blake helped them unhook the fish.

"Is he a keeper?" Lindsey squatted next to the fish that he'd stretched out to measure.

"Can we have him for dinner?" Teddy leaned in close and was petting the fish. Blake had to wonder if Teddy wanted him for dinner or as a pet.

Blake put the bass on the line and measured. He shook his head. "He's not quite big enough."

"Can I toss him back in?" Teddy had hold of the fish with both hands. "And he'll get bigger and I'll catch him again someday."

"I think that's a great idea." Blake happened to make eye contact with Jana. "But first you should let Jana pet him. She looks like she might be feeling left out."

Teddy turned, still holding the fish that was trying to flop its way out of his hands. "You want to pet him before I toss him back?"

Jana shook her head.

Teddy gave her a *girls are silly* look. "He's just a little old fish."

"And he smells like a fish," Jana informed the boy.

"Because he is one." Teddy shook his head at the complexities of women and gave her one last look. "You don't want to pet him?"

"No, but thank you for offering." Jana smiled like she meant it.

If things had been different, they might have had a son by now. But Blake knew it wouldn't do any good to think about that. They *didn't* have a son. They *weren't* married.

He returned to his seat at the front of the boat and guided them away from the bank, back to deeper waters.

He guessed he was in deep enough, though.

Jana offered to make hamburgers since the fishing didn't go as well as expected. Teddy took offense at that. He'd done his part, catching a big old bass. But then he'd agreed that burgers would be good.

She had found premade hamburger patties in the freezer. That meant when Blake came in from the barn with the kids, he could put them on the grill. She'd also found frozen fries, and she'd already preheated the oven and put the cookie sheet of fries in to bake.

It all seemed perfect, like a family having dinner together after a long day on the lake.

But it wasn't perfect. And they weren't a family. The sick feeling in the pit of her stomach was the result of finding the letter Blake had given her days ago. She'd shoved it in her purse, and tonight she would have to read it. She needed to know the details of their divorce.

The back door opened. She listened to Blake telling the kids to wash up in the utility room. Lindsey said something about the pony, and Teddy wanted to know if he could ride it sometime, maybe. Her heart squeezed at the hopeful tone in his voice. She remembered when Lindsey used to beg her to ride horses. Every chance she got, Lindsey wanted riding lessons and she wanted on any horse she could find.

In Africa, in Holland, in Spain, Lindsey had always managed to find horses. She was a Cooper, through and through.

And then the three of them, Blake, Lindsey and Teddy tumbled into the kitchen, all smiles. They looked windblown, a little pink from the sun, but happy. Jana smiled at them, her attention holding on Teddy, because his life was about to be turned upside down. She was sure of it. Blake noticed her look and came up behind her, hugging her quickly and then moving away.

"He'll be fine."

"Can you put those on the grill?" She nodded and handed him the cookie sheet that she'd put the burgers on.

"Of course I can." Blake shot Lindsey a quick look, and she didn't have to be told.

"Hey, Teddy, let's go see if the dog will fetch a ball I found in the garage." Lindsey winked at her dad and then she and Teddy were out the door.

"What's up?" Blake asked.

"I'll follow you outside." She opened the patio door for him, and he walked out ahead of her. "I have the grill preheated."

"Thanks." He shot her a quick look. "Everything okay?"

She shook her head, watching as he put the burgers on the grill. "No. Wyatt called the house phone and I answered. They talked Teddy's mom into going to the hospital. She checked herself in and they're transferring her to Tulsa. Teddy is going to stay here tonight, but Wyatt is sure that Family Services will be here tomorrow to get him. She has family, but they're in Florida and she doesn't want them to have her kids."

Blake took a seat across from her. "We'll figure something out."

"Is it crazy for me to say I don't want him to go? I mean, I know he doesn't know us, but he could stay here."

"It isn't crazy. I'll see if I can get him and

Sissy placed with Mom for now. We'll figure something out."

"If we…" She stopped because she knew she had to tell him.

"What?" And then he grinned. "Don't worry—the same thought crossed my mind. We could take him. But we can't. We have enough to get through without adding two more kids to the mix. Remember, he's part of a set."

"I know." She closed her eyes, wishing, no praying that life could be easier.

"We make pretty decent friends, Jana." He looked as if he was about to say more, but laughter warned that they were about to be invaded by kids.

Sure enough, Lindsey and Teddy came running around the corner of the house, the dog running ahead of them, a stick in his mouth. Teddy fell down on the ground, laughing, and Sam, the dog, turned and dropped his stick. The dog licked the little boy's cheeks and then ran off with his stick again.

They ate a crazy meal with laughter and talking. Jana sipped hot tea, worrying about more than the letter, more than Teddy. She closed her eyes once, swallowing past the tightness in her throat. When she opened her eyes, Blake was watching.

"Teddy, do you want to spend the night here?"

Jana smiled big, making it sound like an adventure. She hoped. "You and Lindsey can put blankets in the family room and watch movies?"

"My mom might not like that."

"She said it will be okay. For tonight. Okay?"

"Is she still sick?" he asked with five-year-old eyes big and worried.

"She isn't feeling very good. She's going to a doctor to see if she can get better."

"For her headache?"

"Yes." Jana smiled and opened her arms to a little boy who hurried into her embrace. "She's going to get better and we're going to help her."

"Okay, I'll watch a dinosaur movie." He hugged her with sweaty, pudgy arms and then he was out of her embrace and heading for the house as if he always spent the night. "Come on, Lindsey."

Lindsey rolled her eyes, but she got up and went after him. She was twelve. Jana was so glad her daughter got to be twelve. She was glad they were going to have more mother-daughter moments to share. Even if it wouldn't be easy.

She was glad to be back in Dawson. She would find a way to make this her home. She thought she might always feel like an outsider, but if Blake was right, if they could be friends, things would get easier.

After Blake left she curled up on the sofa in

the living room with the dog at her feet. Sam liked being an inside dog. She doubted Blake would be happy about the transition from farm dog to house pet.

Blake. She reached for her purse and pulled out the envelope he'd given her at the Mad Cow.

For several days she'd meant to open it. She'd put it off, needing a few days to accept whatever was inside. Before she made plans to return to Dawson she'd thought about how it would feel to face Blake and find out they were divorced.

She'd thought about knocking on his door and being met by a new wife, a new family. How would they have felt to have Blake's daughter suddenly in their lives? She'd even let herself consider that maybe he hadn't divorced her.

There had been a thread of hope that he would be waiting for her, ready to take her back and make them a family again. She had known it was too much to hope for, but she hadn't stopped herself from dreaming.

The letter was the reality. She sighed as she held it up. From the family room she heard the television playing a dinosaur movie. Teddy laughed.

Her hands shook as she slipped a finger under the seal of the envelope to open it. She was mourning a relationship that had ended years ago. She hadn't expected it to hurt like this. Deep down hurt.

Their marriage was over. She had done this to them. She needed to look at this document, to finally see it in black and white. She pulled the papers out of the envelope, her vision blurry.

She read the letter once, then twice, unsure of how to deal with what she was reading. She reached for her tea and let her gaze slide over the words again. From the hallway she heard little feet heading her way. She refolded the papers and slipped them back inside the envelope as Teddy ran through the door, a pillow and blanket held close.

He curled up next to her and within minutes he slept. Sleep didn't come as easily for Jana.

Chapter Nine

Blake showed up at his place early. *His place.* He stepped out of the truck and looked at the house that he'd lived in alone for close to eleven years. In the short time she'd been back it had already morphed into Jana's house. When he walked through the front door, it would smell like candles, coffee and her perfume. He knew it. And he knew the strange things that would happen to his stomach when he smelled those things.

She'd called him bright and early and asked him to stop by if he got a chance. He had chores to do before he headed to the office, so stopping by wasn't a problem.

He found her on the back patio drinking a cup of coffee and watching the sunrise. He sat down next to her and she poured him a cup without asking.

So, did he break the silence or should he give it a few minutes? He didn't remember her as a morning person so he sipped his coffee and gave it time. The kids were obviously still sleeping.

"Well? Is there something you want to talk about?" he finally asked her as he refilled his cup.

Jana tensed. She nearly spilled her coffee as she grabbed an envelope off the table. He recognized it as the envelope from the lawyer. The envelope with their divorce papers. He wondered what she'd found in the documents that would have her so shaken.

Because of her absence he'd filed for custody of Lindsey. He should have discussed that with Jana before now. "Jana, I'm not taking Lindsey from you. I filed for custody but with things the way they are, there is no way I'd put our daughter through that. I won't separate the two of you."

"Blake, that isn't it." She swallowed, and he watched as she slid the paper from the envelope, her hands trembling, making the paper shake.

He took it from her, but he wasn't too eager to read it. He opened the papers and read over the documents. And if an asteroid had crashed into

Oklahoma, he wouldn't have been more shaken than he was as he read through the paperwork.

"I don't understand, Blake." Jana leaned a little toward him.

"It's an affidavit that I should have signed. I'm not sure how I got this again. I thought I signed it so Davis could go to court for me."

He looked over the papers once more, because they obviously weren't divorce papers.

"So if he went to court, we are divorced?"

"Of course. I think he probably sent me the wrong papers. He had a stroke around the time we were finishing up." Blake read through the paper again. "I'll call his son and have him find the right paperwork and send it to us."

"So what does this mean?"

"It means nothing. I'm sure things were settled." He folded the paper and shoved it back in the envelope and then reached for his coffee. Good, strong, black coffee.

"Blake, what did you mean about custody of Lindsey?" Jana's voice shook.

"We've already gone over that. I'm not going to take her from you."

"Thank you."

"But we'll have to get something worked out, maybe joint custody. And I'll pay you child support, of course."

She nodded and then shook her head. "You don't have to do that. I still have money."

"Enough?"

"I'm going to get a job as soon as Lindsey is ready."

"I think it might be a while before she's ready. What happened to your trust fund?"

Jana refilled her coffee and added more to his. He waited. He was good at waiting.

She finally looked up. "Bad investments. My solicitor in London made bad investments. And I had Lindsey's hospital bills."

"We'll make sure the medical expenses are taken care of here in Tulsa. And if you want, I can look at your portfolio and see if we can make better investments." It made him feel more in control, this conversation. He could handle investments. He could handle finances.

He didn't know how to handle the reality that he and Jana might not be divorced. Worse, it meant going through it all over again. And this time, with Lindsey there to witness it all. It had been easy to divorce a wife who had left him and taken their daughter.

Now, with that wife sitting next to him, he wasn't sure how easy it would be.

"I need to make some phone calls now." He finished the lukewarm coffee and stood. "How's Teddy?"

"He slept on the couch with me. Have you heard anything about his mom?"

"No, but I'll give Wyatt a call and see if he has any new information. I did talk to my folks, and they're willing to take Teddy and Sissy."

"I'm willing, too. I'm just not sure what I need to do."

"You'll have to get licensed as a foster parent. And I know they'd be more than willing to have you."

"I'll do whatever I have to do."

He studied her face, wondering how she'd become this woman. She'd taken his daughter away from him. Now she wanted to take in extra children and give them a loving home.

"I'll call you later, after I talk to the lawyer."

She nodded, and he almost leaned to kiss her goodbye. But he couldn't. In his mind they'd been divorced for years. An unsigned piece of paper didn't undo that fact.

On his way to the barn he made the call to the law firm that had handled the divorce and waited while the secretary found Davis Parks, the lawyer. Eventually the other man came on the phone.

"Blake, what can I do for you?"

"Davis, I think I might have messed up ten years ago."

There was a slight pause. "How so?"

Blake stood outside the barn. The mare and her foal walked up to the fence, and he reached absently to stroke the horse's neck.

"I got an affidavit in the mail from your dad, and I never opened it. I guess I was distracted... I don't know. For some reason I thought I'd signed the affidavit and that the divorce was final. When I got the envelope in the mail I didn't want to read it. I didn't want to see that my marriage had ended."

"So what you have is an unsigned affidavit and not the divorce decree?"

"Exactly. I know I should have opened it. I just..."

"Yeah, I know it can be tough. Blake, I'm going to have to research this. I know your divorce was right around the time my dad had his stroke and we also had a staff change. I'll look into it for you."

"I'm sure he went to court." Blake settled on that thought and the strange reaction in his gut. "I just don't want to go through this again. Not now. Jana is back in Oklahoma."

"So we'd have to go through the whole process with her and the child involved?"

"Yes, we would." Blake leaned against the fence. The mare nibbled at his sleeve and then walked away. "Our daughter is sick. This isn't the best scenario."

"I'm sure it isn't. Blake, I'm sorry. With everything happening at that time, I lost track of Dad's cases."

"It isn't your fault."

"I'll look into it for you." He didn't say anything for a minute. "Blake, sometimes things happen for a reason."

How did he answer that? He chose not to. He chose to ignore the comment, ignore the strange sense of wrongs being righted.

He ended the call and walked away from the fence. He heard a truck and stopped at the door of the barn. His dad's truck rolled up the drive.

Tim Cooper stepped down from the truck looking like a man with a full day's work ahead of him. He wore his typical jeans, button-up shirt and the white hat he favored. A lot of men moved to the country and tried farming on for size. Tim Cooper had been country his whole life. He'd raised his children country.

It was a family tradition.

"Dad?"

"Blake." Tim looked around. He watched the mare and her mouse dun foal. Yeah, the filly had thick, foal hair now, but in time she'd be a pretty gray-brown, the color of a mouse. "Pretty baby."

"Yeah, she is."

"How's Jana settling in?" Tim walked up to the fence to watch the mare and foal.

"She isn't settling in my house. I'll help her find a place in town."

"Is that what you want?"

Blake didn't know what to say. He'd never been one to lie to his dad. He also wasn't generally the son who wanted to share every detail of his life.

"We've got a problem with the divorce."

His dad waited.

"It seems I didn't sign an affidavit for Davis to go to court."

"Since I don't speak lawyer, you might have to fill me in."

"Jana and I might not be divorced."

Silence hung between them for a good long while. His dad finally scratched his chin and then he grinned.

"Well, I guess God does have his own way of working things out."

"I'm not sure that's the way I planned on working it out. And this doesn't mean the divorce isn't final. It could be I didn't get the divorce decree, but Davis will find it and send it to me."

"It could be." His dad stepped away from the fence. "I came over here to get that roping saddle you haven't been using. I'm going to help out at Camp Hope, teaching kids to rope."

"You've been talking about that for a while."

His dad shrugged and reached for the door. "Sometimes it takes a man a while to get things right."

Blake followed his dad to the tack room midway down the barn. "That's a pretty big hint."

His dad laughed as he flipped on the light and walked into the room that smelled of leather and hay. "Yeah, I guess it wasn't subtle. I'm not a big fan of Jana's. She took my granddaughter away, and that's not an easy thing to forgive. But I'm also a man who can admit when a person has changed. I think she's changed."

That was all his dad had to say about it. Tim Cooper was a man of few words, always had been.

Blake watched his dad leave with the saddle, and he went back to the barn. He didn't disagree. Jana had changed. They'd both grown up, and both probably realized a few things about life and about themselves.

Did that mean they should just go back to where they'd left off? He didn't see how. If they'd been the same people living the same lives, they would go back and make the same mistakes.

As older, wiser people with some experience

under their belts, it would be like a new relationship with a different person.

But the past was still there, Blake thought, and the past was a hard thing to let go of.

Blake, Jana and Lindsey drove Teddy to Cooper Creek that afternoon. He got out of the truck, but his hand immediately sought Jana's. She smiled down at him, hoping to reassure him. It had been difficult, explaining to him that his mom needed to stay with doctors for a while and that he was going to live with Tim and Angie Cooper.

He'd asked why he couldn't stay with them and they could be his family until his mom got back. She'd hugged him and promised she would be there to see him and he could visit. She'd caught Blake watching her, and she'd known he doubted as much as Teddy.

Angie Cooper met them at the front door. She smiled at the little boy holding tight to Jana. He reached for Lindsey with his other hand.

"Teddy, I'm so glad you're back." Angie bent her knees and sank to his level. "I'm going to make cookies. Do you want to see your room or help me make cookies?"

He bit down on his lip and looked from Lindsey to Angie. "Is Lindsey going to help me make cookies?"

"Of course she can help. And Sissy is here, too. She got here an hour ago, and she's been wondering when you would show up. She has the room right next to yours."

And that's all it took for the little boy to be won over. Angie accepted Blake's outstretched hand, and he helped her to her feet. Teddy dropped Jana's hand and followed Lindsey and Angie through the house. Jana listened to his excited chatter as he told about a kitten he'd seen in the barn and the pony that he thought he might get to ride someday.

"Are you okay?" Blake reached for her hand, and she slipped her fingers through his.

She nodded, because opening her mouth would create a storm of tears that she didn't want to give in to. Teddy would be fine. She knew he would. He would be with Tim and Angie. They would love him and keep him safe. His mother would get better.

Jana felt broken, though. She felt broken for a little boy whose life was falling apart, and she felt broken because her own daughter had been a child whose life fell apart. All of those emotions were swirling, getting confused because of a little boy she barely knew, because he needed them and for some reason they needed him, too.

"It's okay to cry." Blake whispered the words close to her ear.

She couldn't answer, but she turned into his arms and he held her as she cried for children whose parents can't always be what a child needs.

"Teddy is tough and he knows we'll be here for him. A caseworker will come by later, and they'll talk to him and help him understand."

Jana nodded against his shoulder, wiping at her eyes as she tried to get her emotions back in control. Blake's hand stilled on her back and he leaned, dropping a kiss on her temple. She looked up, to tell him something that didn't matter, and his lips found hers. The kiss, gentle and sweet, filled her heart, and somehow she felt broken pieces coming back together.

Something triggered in her brain, telling her to go slowly because Blake wasn't feeling what she felt. He meant to make sure their divorce was final. She wanted forever with a man she'd never stopped loving. She pulled back and took a deep breath.

"I'm sorry," she whispered, afraid to look up and see what might be in his eyes.

"Don't be. It's been a long day already."

His phone buzzed. He gave her an apologetic look and pulled it from his pocket. And then he made long eye contact with her and put it to his ear. Tightness spread across her chest as she watched him. He walked down the steps away from her and she wondered why. If the call was from the lawyer, it was a call that affected them both.

His back was to her. She watched from the porch as he nodded and then glanced back at her. She waited, no longer feeling whole. No longer feeling the sweetness of his kiss.

He slipped the phone into his pocket and walked back up the steps to join her on the porch. She wanted to walk away, to go in the house and bake cookies with the children. She wanted to not hear what he had to say.

"That was Davis."

"And?" Her heart hammered hard against her ribs and it hurt to breathe.

"The divorce was never finalized. Between his dad's stroke and employee changes, it seems things were shuffled and lost. I should have paid more attention. I'm a lawyer—I should have made sure. I was just so tired of it all by then."

"Okay. So what do we do?"

He looked away from her, giving her a sweet view of his strong profile. "He wanted us in there tomorrow. He feels terrible and wants to get this done for us."

"Oh." She didn't know why it hurt so much to hear those words. By all rights her marriage had ended ten years ago.

Blake stood and looked down at her, not smiling. "I told them we'll deal with it later. I think Lindsey needs time to adjust. I don't see how we can do this without her knowledge, and I think we need to explain to her what we're doing and why. But we need to know that she's strong enough."

A strange hopefulness sparked. Jana didn't know what to do with that odd lightness. Blake wasn't going to let it go. It wasn't as if he was giving them a chance. She shouldn't be feeling hopeful, not when he was determined to end their marriage once and for all.

He was giving her a reprieve, that's all.

"We should go back inside," he said in a tone that didn't let her inside his emotions.

"Yes, of course."

They were still married. She tried to process the information even as Blake seemed to be taking it in stride, as if it didn't really matter. It was another business deal he had to take care of, another contract to finalize.

Was that what he truly thought? She reached for his arm, meaning to stop him and ask him.

He stopped when she touched his arm. Looking down at her, he shook his head. As if he knew what she planned to ask him.

"Jana, in my mind we've been divorced for ten years."

"Of course." She shrugged and managed a

smile. "You're right. This is a paper we need to sign. Nothing has changed."

But it should have felt empty, not hopeful. It shouldn't have made her feel as if God had given her this precious gift. Two precious gifts. Lindsey would get better. She and Blake weren't divorced.

She had a second chance. Whatever that meant. Maybe it was a chance to prove to him that she wouldn't run the minute things got difficult. Maybe this meant she had the opportunity to show him they were meant to be together.

Chapter Ten

They left Cooper Creek with a container of still-warm chocolate chip cookies. Sissy and Teddy had waved from the front porch, Blake's mom standing behind them, a hand on each of them. She'd been smiling big. Blake always thought there would come a day when she'd want a break from having a houseful of kids. So far it hadn't happened. She'd taken in Jesse's stepdaughter for a while and Gage's teenage brother-in-law was a constant guest at Cooper Creek.

When they pulled up to his place, Jana got out without saying too much. She looked pale and shaken. He wanted to tell her he would do anything to go back and start over. An unsigned paper didn't change what had happened, though.

It didn't, he repeated to himself. But it was

getting harder to believe. Jana was walking up to the house, their daughter was in the yard playing with the dog. Everything he'd known about his life for ten years was suddenly undone because of one unsigned paper.

He got out of the truck.

"I'm going to the barn. But I'll stop in before I leave."

She smiled but the gesture didn't change the sadness in her eyes. "Okay."

"Can I go with Dad?" Lindsey tossed the tennis ball in her hand, and Sam went after it.

"If your dad doesn't mind." Jana looked to him for an answer.

"Of course she can go with me."

Jana nodded and went inside. He would check on her before he left. A thought clicked in his brain. He didn't know a lot about depression, but he needed to know that she was okay.

"I'm going to put a halter on the foal," he informed Lindsey as they walked toward the barn, knowing she'd love the idea.

"Can I help?" Lindsey looked up, her hazel eyes big and her smile wide.

"I'll get the halter on and you can help me gentle her down a little. We need to get her used to our touch."

He walked into the tack room to get the halter, and he glanced back, watching his daughter with the mare. The foal nudged his tiny nose up to the door but then backed away before she could touch him. Lindsey smiled at Blake and then went back to petting the mare and trying to coax the foal.

He wasn't looking forward to telling her about the divorce. Not now, when she was getting healthier. Not now, because she was adjusting to her life, to the relationship between her parents. Telling her they were still married but filing for divorce. How would she accept news like that? He looked over the assortment of halters but didn't really see them.

Things were definitely more complicated than they'd been a week ago. A week ago he'd been divorced and building a relationship with his daughter. Today he was a married man again.

Lindsey turned to see what was taking him so long, and he managed a smile, holding up the miniature halter he'd found as he walked out of the tack room, switching off the light on his way out the door.

"It's pink." Lindsey smiled at that. "She'll look good in pink."

"I thought you might like that." He eased through the stall door. "I should have done this sooner, but things have been a little hectic around here."

Lindsey leaned on the door, watching him. "Because of me."

"You're a good thing in my life, Lindsey. I'll take hectic all day long if it means having you here."

"Sometimes I'm still really mad at mom." Lindsey reached for the mare, sliding a hand down her neck.

"I guess that's understandable." Blake looked up, a quick glance, not taking too much attention from the mare and foal.

"She should have at least told you where I was."

"She made a mistake. Sometimes people make decisions and then it's hard to go back and undo things."

"I guess," she said without a whole lot of conviction.

He smiled up at her as he smoothed a hand down the neck of the little filly and slid the halter over her head. She pulled away from him, and her momma gave him a mean look, her ears back.

"See how this momma horse doesn't want me to mess with her baby?" He buckled the halter as he talked.

"Yeah. She'd like to kick you."

He had to agree, and he was watching those hind legs as he worked. "Exactly. Moms are protective. Even though I wouldn't hurt this baby for anything, she's not convinced. She'll do whatever it takes to keep her baby safe."

"I guess."

He guessed, too. It hadn't been the example he wanted to make, because the last thing he wanted to do was understand Jana and what she'd done to him. He'd meant for this to help Lindsey understand. But Jana had been protecting her daughter, afraid his last name, his money, would mean he'd take their daughter from her.

"Do you want to pet this baby?" He held the halter, rubbing his hands down the foal's sides. "Jackson has obviously been working with her, too. She's not too shy."

"Can I come in the stall?"

"No, I don't think so. Two of us in here might be too much for her momma. But I'll open the door a little and you can pet her."

Lindsey stepped in the opening and reached for the foal. Her fingers brushed the thick coat and she smiled. "I've always loved horses. I guess I didn't know why."

"You're a Cooper—you can't help yourself. It's in your blood."

"Right, I guess it is." She smiled big, rubbing her hand across the foal's face. "I hope someday I can ride."

"I hope so, too."

The door opened. Lindsey stepped back and he released the foal. He guessed they both looked pretty guilty to Jana as she walked up the aisle between the stalls.

"What are you two up to?" She smiled, but something was missing in that smile.

"Dad put the halter on the baby, and we're petting her, to get her used to people."

"Of course." Jana moved back, allowing him room to step out of the stall.

He had opened the door that allowed the mare access to the corral. The three of them watched the mare and foal leave the barn and then trot across the corral. He would give them a few more days and then turn them out with the other horses. He always liked to keep a new foal up for a time, just to give them a chance to get used to people.

"Ready to go to the house?"

Lindsey didn't look quite ready, but she nodded.

He turned off lights, and the three of them went out the door.

"Are you okay?" he asked Jana as they walked to the house.

"I'm fine. I made pie. Do you want a piece?"

"I'll take some. Do you have ice cream?" It was the wrong answer. He should have told her he had to go home. He had work he needed to catch up on. Those were the right answers, but not the ones he wanted to give.

"I think you have ice cream in the freezer." Jana walked next to him. "I thought we could talk about Lindsey's birthday."

Lindsey heard that. She came back to walk with them. "I already know what I want."

"What's that?" Blake asked as they walked.

"It's a secret. Something I've been praying for."

Her answer gave him a bad feeling. "We can't get what you want if you don't share."

She shot him a secretive smile and bounded off with the dog, tossing back over her shoulder. "If I told, it wouldn't be a secret. Don't worry, I've got this covered."

Jana laughed a little. "She's obviously feeling good."

"Doesn't that answer worry you a little, though?"

Jana shrugged. "Maybe a little. What if she's praying for a pet monkey? Or a tiger?"

He thought it probably had more to do with two parents being reunited. But he didn't share that with Jana.

Lindsey beat them to the house. When they walked through the door of the kitchen, she was cutting pie and placing it on big plates. Jana shook her head but didn't stop her daughter from giving them the gigantic pieces she'd cut.

Instead she pulled ice cream out of the freezer and put it on the counter for Lindsey to scoop. Blake watched the two of them. She felt it. She shivered a little, chilled from the cool air inside after being in the heat outside. Or that's what she'd been telling herself. She couldn't be sick.

"Okay, you're not going to tell us what you're praying for. But what about a party?" Blake asked as he took a seat at the island in the center of the kitchen.

"I want a big party with all of my Cooper family," Lindsey informed them and then she licked chocolate off her fingers. Jana handed her a paper towel. "And I want a slumber party with my cousins. I have a lot of time to make up for."

"Lindsey, I'm so sorry you haven't had those things."

Lindsey looked up from the ice cream she'd been scooping onto the plates. "I didn't say that to make you feel bad. It's just a fact, Mom. Now that we're here, I have a lot of time to make up for."

"I know you do." Jana sat down at the table, afraid of the way she felt. She looked up, and Blake was watching her, his eyes narrowed.

He looked so good. She thought about how it would feel if he gathered her up in his arms right then and there and held her tight. And that meant she must have a fever. The last thing they needed to do was give Lindsey false hope, especially if they were going to have to drag her through a divorce.

"Lindsey, why don't you take your pie to your room?" Blake said it with a soft, quiet voice.

"Why? Grown-up talk, right? I had a friend who always complained that her parents would send her to her room when they wanted to fight. Are you going to fight?"

Jana met her daughter's curious and hopeful look. "No, we're not going to fight."

"Oh." She seemed almost disappointed. "I just thought it would be cool to be sent to my room so my parents could fight."

"Just go. And tell your mom goodbye." Blake's voice, his seriousness, caught their daughter's attention. She picked up her plate and shot Jana a curious look.

"Blake, let's not get dramatic." Jana tried but her head felt fuzzy.

"You're sick." He said it in a way that made it sound like an accusation.

"I know."

"Oh." Lindsey headed for the door with her plate. "See you later, Mom."

"I love you, Lindsey." Jana called after her daughter's retreating back. And then she looked up at Blake. "I'm sorry."

"Why? You're sick, Jana. It happens. But it isn't something you should hide." He pulled out a chair and sat next to her.

"I'm used to always being with her, taking care of her."

"I get that. But I'm here, and you taking care of her is not an option. Not if you're sick." He placed a strong, tanned hand on her cheek, and she closed her eyes at the touch, the gentle touch with his work-roughened hands that felt so cool on her face. She'd always loved his hands.

"Jana."

She opened her eyes and he shook his head. She'd loved having his hand on her cheek. He looked as if he hadn't been moved, not a bit. Instead he looked concerned.

"I'm sick." She sighed and leaned back in the chair, brushing her hair back from her face.

"You feel pretty warm."

"What do we do?"

"You go to Cooper Creek and stay in the apartment over the barn. I'll stay here. I'll get things cleaned, disinfected, and you can rest and get better."

"What if you get sick?"

"I don't get sick." He smiled a confident smile as he said it. "And having a day or two to rest up will be good for you. You have to take care of yourself." That concern again. But it wasn't for her, it was for Lindsey, wasn't it?

Maybe she should go, though. Distance between them, even from one house to another would be a good thing.

"Okay. I'll pack a bag and go."

"I'll call my folks and let them know you're on your way over. And I'll call Jesse to come over and check Lindsey. What symptoms do you have, other than the fever?"

"I feel weak and my throat has been scratchy."

He glanced at his watch. "I'll have someone pick you up. You don't need to drive."

"Blake, I can take care of myself." She hadn't meant for her voice to sound harsh. He didn't seem to be bothered by her tone.

"Jana, the last thing we need is for you to get in a wreck."

"Of course, you're right." She pushed herself up from the table, and her legs felt weaker than they had earlier. She really didn't have time to be sick. She started to tell Blake but her eyes lost focus.

Strong arms went around her, pulling her close and then lifting her off the ground. She leaned against his shoulder as he carried her to the living room and placed her on the sofa. When he sat next to her she opened her eyes and looked up.

"I didn't mean to get sick," she whispered.

"People rarely do." He smiled a soft smile and smoothed her hair, his fingers remaining at her temple, stroking softly.

"I should go."

"Yes, you should."

"I'd rather crawl in my own bed and stay here."

He pulled her close, cradling her against his solid body. His arms were holding her, the way she'd wanted. Because she was sick, she reminded herself. Her fever-fogged brain had enough sense to remind her that he was just being kind.

His hand stroked her arm and his lips touched the top of her head. And then he stood up. "Let me call Jesse and see what he says."

She closed her eyes, nodding. A blanket slipped over her shoulders and she heard his retreating steps on the hardwood floor. She shivered into the blanket, alone and worried. How had something hit this suddenly? She'd been fine earlier. Maybe a little scratchy-throated, but not sick.

Footsteps returned. She opened her eyes and looked up to see Blake standing next to the sofa. He sat down on the edge of the seat and handed her a glass of water and pills.

"This should help."

She swallowed the pills. "What did Jesse say?"

"He said to quarantine you in your bedroom. I'll stay here tonight, and we'll see how things are tomorrow. He wants to check you for strep."

"Okay," she whispered, and snuggled back into the blanket.

"Uh-uh, you have to go to bed."

She looked up at him. "You're right."

"Come on, let's go." He held out a hand and she took it, letting him pull her to her feet.

He led her down the hall to her room. His room. The room they had once shared. When they'd been married. Oh, wait, they were still married. She started to remind him of that but thought it might be a bad idea.

"Lindsey needs to eat and take her meds," Jana whispered as she crawled into bed, the blankets already pulled back.

"I think I can handle that." Blake spoke from the doorway. "I'll bring you another glass of water. If you need anything, I'm just in the other room."

Need. She started to open her mouth and tell him she needed him to hold her again. She needed to find a way to make him love her again. If he'd just forgive her.

But she didn't say any of those things.

"Go to sleep, Jana." His voice sounded faraway.

"Blake?"

He stepped back into the room. She saw his dark form standing with the light of the hall behind him. "Yes?"

"Thank you for staying."

"You're welcome."

The door closed, and she was alone in the dark room. Alone with her thoughts. And those thoughts were more dangerous than ever before.

Later, when the fever broke, she would face reality. Blake Cooper had forgiven her. He could be kind to her. But he didn't love her. And this mistake with the divorce didn't mean that they would stay married, that they would raise Lindsey together.

Jana would be thirty-five soon. She was no longer a young girl, or even a young woman who allowed herself to get caught up in romantic fantasy. Her life was about harsh reality. Her husband still wanted a divorce and her daughter would still face challenges.

The medicine he'd given her must have been working because she was starting to feel better. And it made her heart ache worse than anything else.

Chapter Eleven

Blake woke up in a new world Friday morning. He rolled over on the couch, and Lindsey was looking down at him. The ache in his lower back reminded him he was too old and had been thrown from too many horses to sleep on a couch. He stretched and smiled at his daughter.

"It's about time." She grinned and plopped down in the nearby rocking chair.

"What time is it?"

"Six."

He groaned and raised his arm to look at his watch. "Why are you up so early?"

"We have chores. Right? Isn't that what farm people do?"

He noticed she was dressed in jeans, a T-shirt and boots. Somewhere she'd found a cowboy hat that fit. Barely. It was white straw and slipped down over her forehead a little too far, making her face seem even smaller.

"Yes," he managed with a smile, "we have chores."

"So get up. I had cereal for breakfast. Mom is still sleeping."

"You need to stay out of her room." Blake sat up, running a hand through his hair and then across his cheek. He had clothes here but nothing to shave with.

"I didn't go in…I peeked. Anyway, I've already been around her," his daughter stated with a matter-of-fact tone that he normally wouldn't have argued with.

"Right, but we're not taking any chances."

A car pulled up the drive. His brother, Dr. Jesse Cooper, bright and early as usual. Another groan as Blake stood, found his socks and boots and headed for the front door.

"Do you always creak when you walk?"

He shot his daughter a look. "Not usually."

"There's another bedroom."

"I know. I fell asleep reading."

"Oh. Do you want me to make coffee?"

He opened the door for Jesse, but his daughter's previous statement caught his attention. "You make coffee?"

"I'm almost thirteen. I used to drink coffee." She said it with a little bit of a sad voice. "You know, you're not supposed to drink a lot of coffee, either."

"I promise I won't. I have a single-serve coffeemaker, and I think I also have herbal tea and hot cocoa you can make with it."

Her smile returned. "Thanks. I'll go turn it on."

Jesse had made it to the front door while Blake had been talking to his daughter. Obviously Jesse had been up for a while, too. He was dressed for a day at the hospital and he'd shaved. Blake felt more than a little scruffy.

"Are you the patient?" Jesse grinned as he walked through the front door.

"No, but I feel like one."

"I'll check you over before I leave, just to make sure you don't have what Jana has. There's a virus going around, so I don't think she'll be sick for more than a few days."

"What about Lindsey?" Blake walked with his brother through the house.

"Hopefully she doesn't get it. But she is going to get sick, Blake. Maybe not this time, but eventually. Over time, her body will get stronger and be able to fight it better."

Blake heard a crash from the kitchen and an "Uh-oh."

Jesse laughed. "That doesn't sound good."

"No, it doesn't. She was going to turn on the coffeemaker."

"Well, coffee isn't the best thing for you, anyway."

In answer Blake shot Jesse a dirty look.

They walked into the kitchen, and Lindsey looked up from the mess she was sweeping up. "I dropped a cup."

"It sounded worse." Blake looked around the kitchen. He surveyed the dark-haired minx that was his daughter. Man, he really loved her. "Did you cut yourself?"

"No, and if I did, it wouldn't hurt the kidney." She frowned and went back to sweeping.

"Linds, not everything is about the kidney. I wanted to make sure you're okay."

Tears hovered in her hazel eyes, and she managed a watery smile. "I know. I just don't want everything in my life to be about kidneys."

"I'm afraid you're going to have to give that some time," Jesse offered. "Eventually things will settle down. Rejection will be less of a risk. But, Lindsey, this is always going to be your life. You're going to have to live a different life than most people. You're going to be on medication. You're going to have to take precautions."

"Yeah, I know." She dumped the broken pieces from the dustpan into the trash. "So, I guess you'd better make sure my mom is okay."

Jesse nodded and left the kitchen, leaving Blake with his daughter.

"I'm having herbal tea." Blake put the plastic pod in the coffeemaker. "How about you?"

She smiled a little and hopped up on the bar stool at the counter. "If you are, I am."

He made two cups of tea and then he picked one that he thought would be good for his sick wife. Ex-wife. He shook his head as he set the cup under the spout. Man, life was about as complicated as it could get. Two days ago she'd been his ex-wife. Today she was still his wife.

"Why are you frowning at the coffeemaker?" Lindsey asked as she poured sugar in her tea.

"Just thinking that I'd rather have coffee, but I'm following your very good example."

Again she smiled. "Do you think we should make Mom chicken soup? It's supposed to be healthy."

"I think we could manage. Later, after those chores you insist we need to do."

Jesse returned a few minutes later. He washed his hands at the sink and dried them on a paper towel. "From her symptoms I think it's the virus everyone is catching. But it's still good if Lindsey keeps her distance until Jana is fever-free for twenty-four hours."

For a few minutes they talked, and Blake

thought he was in the clear. Until Jesse pulled a thermometer out of his bag.

"Let me look at your throat and check your temp. I'm going to check Lindsey's, too." Jesse came after him with a stick that he insisted on gagging him with.

"Are you trying to choke me?" Blake managed, after the stick was removed from his throat. Lindsey was laughing and he gave her a warning look. "Don't laugh too loud, I think you're next."

"It isn't in your throat, Dad. It's just a tongue depressor."

Jesse chuckled. "She has you there."

"Of course she does. I've learned I'm almost never right anymore."

"Welcome to my world," Jesse said in a dry tone, but with a big smile, because he was married now and had a young stepdaughter.

"How's Laura doing?"

"Pregnant and hungry."

Blake started to say that he remembered what that was like, but the words and the memories were too much. Jesse went on, checking Lindsey, and then he made himself a cup of coffee.

"The two of you are good to go. But if you do start to feel sick, let me know." Jesse stood at the counter watching them. "Everything else is okay?"

"Of course it is."

Lindsey shrugged a little. "We're going out to do chores in a few minutes and then we're going to make chicken soup for my mom."

"I would recommend you call Vera and have her make the chicken soup."

Blake took offense at that. "I can cook."

"Burgers on the grill, chicken on the grill, vegetables on the grill." Jesse winked at Lindsey. "Do we see a pattern?"

"Don't you have a job to go to?" Blake asked as he finished his tea and set the cup in the sink. He knew he had a job to go to. And most likely the best plan was to work from home again. Jesse stood, and Blake walked with him to the front door.

"Keep an eye on Jana," Jesse said as they walked out the door.

"An eye on her? I thought she was okay, just a virus."

"I'm talking about depression, Blake. I think she's fine, but since she has dealt with this in the past…" Jesse shrugged. "This has been a rough situation for her. If you start to notice symptoms of depression, you need to make sure she sees a doctor."

Of course. He'd shared with his mother. She'd shared with Jesse. He doubted she would spread it too far, but she would have thought Jesse needed to know.

His mind raced back to symptoms he should have noticed all of those years ago. He should have noticed that she stopped cleaning. She stopped caring how she looked. He thought it was about him, about their relationship or about her being homesick for England.

"Don't be so hard on yourself," Jesse offered. "Or on her."

"I take it you've heard the news."

They were at Jesse's car. "About the divorce. Yes, I heard."

"I never expected this."

"No, I guess you didn't. You'll figure out what to do."

Yeah, he guessed he would. But it wouldn't be easy. None of this was easy, and to complicate things, he knew he had a daughter praying for her family to be whole. She wasn't wishing on shooting stars; she was holding on to faith. The faith of a child.

And Blake knew that a child's faith could move mountains.

Jana awoke to the smell of something wonderful cooking. The aroma drifted under the closed door. So did the sounds of Blake's voice, low and rumbling, and Lindsey's higher-pitched laughing. Jana didn't move. She wanted to bask in the sounds of her daughter's happiness.

It had been the right thing, to bring her back. She should have brought her back years ago. No, she shouldn't have left in the first place.

The door opened. It was late afternoon and the sun streamed in the window. Blake peeked around the corner of the door and then he stepped inside, carrying a tray. Lindsey stood in the hall behind him, waving. Jana blew her daughter a kiss.

"We made chicken soup," Lindsey called out from the hall.

Blake shook his head as he set the tray on the table next to the bed. "She's impossible and full of energy today."

"She shouldn't get…"

Blake held up a hand. "She took a long nap. Don't worry…I'm taking care of her."

"I know you are." But it had been so long since someone else had taken care of her daughter. Jana corrected herself. Their daughter. Lindsey was their daughter. Of course Blake could take care of her.

"Are you hungry?" Blake put a spoon in the bowl.

"Starving. The toast at lunch seemed like plenty, but now I'm hungry."

"You're getting better. Jesse said it was just a two-or three-day virus."

"I'm so glad. I don't want to miss the rodeo."

His eyes widened in surprise. "Really?"

"Really."

He didn't push it. Instead he moved the tray and situated it over her lap. She tried to push back memories but she couldn't. Blake had always been this way. After she'd had Lindsey, he'd cooked for her. He'd cleaned house. He'd taken his turn with late-night feedings.

He hadn't noticed her slipping away, though. Maybe he'd thought she would get better. Maybe he'd thought she just needed time.

"Stop."

She looked up, unsure. "What?"

He took a seat in the nearby chair and twisted the blinds to close them against the sun. "You're thinking about the past. I don't know if you're thinking about what we could have done differently, or if you're remembering why you left."

"I'm thinking about how hard you tried to make me happy."

He stood up, moving toward the door. "It didn't work, did it?"

"Blake, don't walk out."

He turned, not smiling. "I'm not."

"You couldn't fix what was happening to me, not on your own."

"I guess I know that." He looked out the door for their daughter.

Jana could hear Lindsey in the living room. She must have turned the television to country music videos, and she was singing. She probably didn't expect a dramatic scene between her parents. If she had, she wouldn't have left.

"Sit down and keep me company?" She motioned to the chair he'd vacated. "I could share my soup."

"Lindsey and I ate an early dinner."

"Soup?"

He laughed at that. "Afraid not. Chicken on the grill. She insisted a sick person needs chicken soup, so we made soup for you."

Together, the two of them in the kitchen. Jana could picture them tossing ingredients in without measuring, laughing, sharing. A little envy washed over her.

"It's really good." She took another spoonful of the soup. "You were always a decent cook."

"Decent?" He smiled as he said it.

"More than decent." She finished the bowl while he sat in the chair, looking more at the wall than at her.

"Are you still cool?" He stood, placing his hand on her forehead.

"Well?" she whispered when he stepped away.

"Still cool. Do you want coffee or iced tea?

I brought you a glass of water, but you might want more than that."

She shook her head. The thing she wanted most was to get up and leave this room. And she wanted him to realize she had never stopped loving him. Maybe if she told him?

But how would that sound? If she told him she left and didn't come back for ten years, but she always loved him? Would he ever believe that?

Maybe he would, but it would just be baggage between them as they proceeded with their divorce.

"Lindsey brushed the pony today," he told her as they sat in the quiet room.

"She's safe doing that, right?"

"I won't let her do anything that might get her hurt."

"Of course you won't."

"She had a good time. She has to have normal moments, Jana. Everything else in her life seems mixed-up and confusing."

Jana thought about the crazy mixed-up life she had created for her daughter. "You're right. But being here, Blake, this is good for her. Your family is good for her."

"No regrets?" he asked, and she wondered where the question came from and if it meant more.

"None." Except maybe treading into this territory of emotion and their lives. "Do you think Teddy could go to the rodeo with us? I don't want him to think we've abandoned him."

"I'm sure he could. Mom called this afternoon. Things aren't good."

She sat up a little more. "What happened?"

"Lisa walked out of the hospital. They're looking for her, but so far..." He shrugged.

"I hate hearing that. If we'd left her alone..."

"What? She wouldn't have gotten better on her own."

"I know." She reached for the water he'd left on the table. "So what happens now?"

"I guess they stay with my folks for a while until a permanent placement is found. And until we can find Lisa and get her help."

"I need to get in touch with Family Services. I really want Teddy and Lisa, Blake." She sighed as the words slipped out. "I'm sorry. This isn't my house."

Blake laced his fingers together on his lap and closed his eyes. "I'm not sure what to do anymore."

That was how he left things. Then he told her he had to move some hay they'd just baled. Lindsey would be in the house if she needed anything.

He walked out, closing the door behind him, leaving her to pray about her life here in Dawson, her marriage and now two little children who sadly needed someone to care for them until their mother was able.

Chapter Twelve

The lights of the rodeo blazed bright around the arena. Blake stood next to the horse Jackson's daughter, Jade, planned to barrel race. The girl had her blond hair back in a ponytail and a white cowboy hat shoved down on her head. She looked as if she'd been on the ranch her whole life. But it had really only been a couple of years.

She moved her leg and he tightened the cinch on the saddle and made sure her stirrups were right for her legs. "You got this, Jade?"

She nodded, moving in the saddle, settling in. "I've got it. I'm winning this one for Lindsey."

Lindsey smiled, moving to stand next to the big golden palomino Jackson had bought Jade for her last birthday. Blake hadn't agreed with the purchase. He'd thought the animal would be too much horse for a girl just starting out. He'd underestimated Jade. When the kid decided to do something, she didn't back down. She and the horse were a formidable team.

And he could tell that Lindsey wanted to be the one riding home on a horse like Jim.

He hoped someday. Maybe not barrels, but on a good broke horse she'd be able to ride and do more of the things she wanted to do.

"I should head for the arena." Jade pulled back on the reins, backing the horse. "Wish me luck."

Lindsey followed for a few feet but then stopped to wait for Blake. "We have to get down there so we can watch."

"Don't worry…we'll watch," Blake promised his daughter. "Where's your mom?"

"Sitting with everyone. She has Teddy and Sissy with her."

"Gotcha. Let me put this brush away, and we'll go find a seat."

"Are you going to ride?" Lindsey followed him to the back of the trailer where he had extra brushes, halters and lead ropes.

"Nope, doctor's orders."

"So you're just not going to ride?"

He smiled down at her. "Linds, I'm not going to take any chances."

She wrinkled her nose at him, but she smiled. "Okay, thanks for being such a great role model.

We should head back to the bleachers so we don't miss Jade's ride. And Lucky's daughter, Sabrina, is riding, too."

"I guess we'd better go cheer on our family."

As they walked toward the risers where the crowds were sitting, he spotted Jana with Teddy and Sissy, one on either side of her. Heather sat on the other side of Sissy, leaning to hear what the little girl was saying. He'd made a trip to check out Heather's new home. She seemed excited about leaving her apartment in Grove and moving closer to family. Some people had never understood her desire to live in Grove, but Blake got it.

The Coopers could be overwhelming. Heather focused on her business and she kept her personal life personal. His gaze connected with Jana's, and he wondered if she would survive being in the middle of their lives once again.

He climbed the bleachers, Lindsey coming up behind him. He took the empty space next to Teddy. Lindsey chose to sit in the front row, close to the fence and the action. Teddy scooted down next to her, and she put an arm around his shoulders, leaning to tell him something.

Even to him they looked like a family. Jana, Sissy, Teddy, Lindsey and himself. It changed his world, that thought. Weeks ago he'd been sitting there envying the people around him who were talking to their kids, watching them grow up on horses. Today his daughter was two rows down from him at a rodeo.

And Jana was sitting next to him, her arm brushing his, the scent of roses blending with dust and horse sweat.

Fortunately for him, the barrel racing event started, taking his mind off the woman at his side and the contentment that he hadn't expected to feel.

"When is Jade up?" Jana asked, leaning close.

"She's fifth. I think Sabrina is second." He made an attempt at studying the girls lined up for the event and he nodded. "Sabrina is up next."

The girl who'd gone first rounded the third barrel and sent the deep red chestnut she rode down the homestretch. Lindsey couldn't help herself. She jumped up and cheered and then sat back down, her cheeks a little pink.

"Wrong team." She smiled back at him.

"I think it's okay to cheer on a good rider," Jana offered, and then she looked up at him. "Isn't it?"

He needed an answer, but her blue eyes froze him and he couldn't think. Man, he really wanted to be eighteen again. At eighteen a guy didn't think about broken hearts and the future. At eighteen it was about today, the moment and nothing more. He wanted to take Jana by the hand, lead her down to the creek and kiss her senseless.

"Blake?" Her voice was breathy, soft.

"Jade's up next," he managed to say.

"Of course." Jana settled back in the seat, and in a few minutes she was drawn into a conversation with Heather.

Blake moved to the seat next to his daughter and Teddy so he could explain Jade's ride to her. Or at least that's what he told himself. When Jade flew out of the gate on the palomino, Lindsey grabbed his hand. The ride was nearly flawless, but the horse came out a little too far on the last barrel. Jade got the animal back on track and almost soared to the finish line. The time was called by the MC of the event. Lindsey jumped up, cheering.

"We have to congratulate them." She looked down at him and was already stepping down off the bleachers.

"We'll head back there in a minute. Maybe your mom and Sissy and Teddy would like to go with us."

Common sense no longer seemed to matter. Jana wasn't his ex-wife; she was his wife. And tonight, in jeans, boots, a sparkly T-shirt and a white cowboy hat, how could he not want to hold her hand.

He wanted to be eighteen and short on common sense.

"Let's get something to eat." Lindsey echoed his thoughts. Kind of.

The rodeo snack bar didn't really serve cotton candy, but he'd settle for a corn dog. He looked up at Jana. "Want to go with us?"

She nodded and slid down to join them. Somehow, Blake ended up in the middle of Lindsey, Jana, Teddy and Sissy. He reached to pick up Teddy, and the little guy wrapped his arms tight around Blake's neck. They walked up to the white painted building that resembled a shed and ordered corn dogs and sodas. Lindsey grabbed the first one, plus a packet of mustard.

"I'm going to go see Jade," she announced.

"Works for me," Blake agreed. "But watch where you're going. We'll be there in a few minutes."

Jana was gazing after their daughter.

"She'll be fine. And there isn't a person here who isn't watching out for her."

"I'm sure someday I'll relax."

"Of course we will." He handed corn dogs to Teddy and then Sissy.

The kids were standing next to the arena when his mom joined them. "I'm here to take Teddy and Sissy home. This is almost over, and I like to get on the road before the crowd."

"Do we have to?" Teddy looked about ready to stomp his foot in a tantrum, but Sissy took him by the hand.

"We have to be good, Teddy," she warned, sounding a lot older than her seven years.

"But I wanted to go home with Lindsey," he insisted.

Blake's mom leaned to talk to him. "Lindsey is pretty busy right now. But I think we'll see her tomorrow after church."

"Are you sure?"

Angie smiled at that. "Pretty sure."

Blake tugged Teddy's hat low. "You go with Nana Angie, and we'll see you tomorrow."

The little boy reached for her hand. "Okay, I guess."

Blake watched them walk away. When Jana's hand found its way into his, he smiled down at her and saw the soft wistfulness in her blue eyes. People moved around them.

Somehow they ended up on the trail to the creek. Maybe he planned it that way. Maybe memories took over and it just happened. They walked side by side, not hand in hand. He was going to kiss her. He didn't see a way in the world that he wouldn't. She was wearing some kind of peach lip gloss, and her eyes were smoky blue this evening, not the lighter blue of a March sky.

Lindsey was with family. He knew she wouldn't miss them for a little while. The noise of the rodeo receded into the background to be replaced by the sound of the creek, tree frogs and an occasional bird.

When they got to the edge of the creek, the air was cooler. The scent of honeysuckle was heavy. Jana tossed her trash in the barrel someone with foresight had chained to a post. Blake did the same.

"I've always loved the smell of honeysuckle."

Blake agreed, but for some reason he couldn't react, couldn't comment. She looked up at him, unsure, beautiful, still as vulnerable as the young woman whose car hadn't started on a spring day all of those years ago.

Moonlight filtered down, capturing them in its silver light. Blake removed the hat Jana wore, and the moon caught in her blond hair. She looked up at him, her lips parting slightly.

Blake leaned, brushing a hand across her cheek as he bent and captured her lips in a soft kiss. She trembled in his arms and he pulled her close, holding her against him as his lips continued to explore hers.

If only he could be angry with her.

But what he felt was anything but anger. What he felt, what he wanted, was to have his wife in his arms forever. He wanted to hold her and to not be afraid that she'd walk away again and take the best part of him with her, leaving him with just half a life.

He paused, his lips still on hers. He tasted the saltiness of her tears, warm on her cool skin.

"What are we doing?" he whispered.

She shook her head, her lips still close to his. She brushed a kiss across his cheek, and her hands moved to his, her fingers interlocking with his fingers.

"I'm not sure what we're doing." She buried her face against his shoulder.

He kissed the top of her head and she looked up again. He touched her lips with another kiss, this one less gentle. He wanted to keep her with him forever, holding her close.

But it wasn't about him, what he wanted. It was about her and what she could do to him if she left again. He would eventually have to tell her that he'd contacted Davis and asked for paperwork that would give him custody of Lindsey if she tried to leave again.

Standing there, with her in his arms, that paperwork felt like an insult. And he knew that's how she would take it if he presented it to her. He either trusted her or he didn't.

"We should go back. Lindsey will be looking for us."

"Blake—" she stepped back, letting go of his hands "—I want to fix us."

He backed against a tree at the edge of the creek and pulled her with him. He leaned down, studying her face, her eyes and the lips he'd kissed moments ago.

She wanted to fix them.

"I'm not perfect, Blake. I'm not going to be perfect. But I'm doing my best to make things right."

"I know you are." He did. At first he'd thought this was only about getting Lindsey the help she needed. Maybe that had been Jana's intention in the beginning.

It had been his intention to help his daughter. He'd had no desire to let his ex-wife back into his life. He leaned in to kiss her again.

She backed away. "No. You have to stop that. I can't think when you do that."

Yeah, well, he couldn't think when she was around, either. His anger with her was disappearing, becoming mostly a memory. Ten years of fear and searching.

Now he had to think about life with them back in his world. She wanted to fix them, and he was still deciding whether to trust or not to trust.

Lindsey was angry. Jana could see it from a distance. Her daughter stood next to a post at the edge of the bleachers, and her features were a tight mask of anger. Jana reached for Blake's hand.

"Something happened."

Blake looked down at her and then glanced toward their daughter. Of course he didn't see what Jana was seeing on her daughter's face. He hadn't the experience. But no doubt Lindsey had the Cooper temper. It took a long time to get one of them pushed to the edge, and they usually got over it quickly, but when they were mad, watch out.

"Why do you think something has happened?"

"Your daughter looks like you when she's mad."

Blake blinked. "When do I get mad?"

If she hadn't been so worried about Lindsey, Jana would have laughed. "Almost never, Blake. But when you do, it's a frightening thing to see. Do you know how badly my legs shook that day I confronted you at the ranch?"

"Do you know how badly I wanted to shake you?"

"Exactly." She released his hand and headed for her daughter. Lindsey had crossed her arms in front of herself and her shoulders were squared.

"What's up, Lindsey Bug?" Blake went for

a lightness that Jana could have told him wouldn't work.

"Why do I find out all of the important stuff from other people?"

"Lindsey, what are you talking about?" Jana slipped an arm around her daughter's very stiff back and headed her toward the truck. She had a feeling they would need privacy.

"Jade asked me if I was glad that my parents are still married."

"Jade did what?" Blake's tone could have cut through steel.

Jana looked back at him, giving him a cautioning look. She turned her attention back to their daughter as they walked toward the truck. "Why did Jade ask you that?"

"Because Jade thought it was a good thing. And if I didn't know better, I would think so, too. But you aren't really married, are you?"

Jana stopped at the truck. She didn't want to get inside. She didn't want to be in close confines with Blake. She also didn't want to be on public display as they dealt with another family drama. It was bad enough, going to church and knowing people talked. At the Mad Cow she saw people whispering behind their hands. Even here, at the rodeo, she had overheard a few conversations. She was the kidnapper who had taken Blake's daughter.

Maybe someday that would change. Maybe someday Blake would stop thinking of her as the person who could walk away again. Sometimes she thought it was happening, that he was giving them a second chance.

The look on his face as his daughter questioned them made her wonder if he'd ever thought about them being together again.

"Lindsey, this is a complicated situation." Blake stood a few feet away from them, and his tone was that father type, the kind that told a child this was too adult for her to understand.

Lindsey heard it, too. "I'm smart, and I do understand what's going on. And if everyone else, even my cousins, knows what is going on, I want to know. I don't want everyone to be talking about my life and my family."

Jana looked at Blake, and he nodded, giving her the go-ahead.

"There was a mistake with the paperwork. Your father did file for divorce, but one of the important documents didn't get signed."

Lindsey's face lit up and she smiled. Jana's heart sank. She didn't want her daughter to have false hope, to believe that birthday prayer would come true.

"So you aren't getting a divorce?" She looked from Jana to Blake and back to Jana.

Jana didn't know what to say to that. She

looked at Blake, and she could tell by his expression that he didn't want to do this anymore than she did. So why were they?

They stood there, the three of them—Jana, Lindsey and Blake, leaning against the truck, staring up at a sky that had grown cloudy. The arena had grown quiet. People were heading for their cars. Horses and other livestock were being loaded. Jana could hear laughter and conversations that were quiet from a distance. And to the south, thunder echoed.

"I'm not a baby. I know you think because I'm sick I can't handle the truth, but I can." Lindsey broke the silence, looking from one to the other of them. "It might not be what I want, but I really don't want to pretend I know when I don't."

"Okay, here's the truth." Blake sighed as he said it. "We were waiting to do this later. We don't want to hurt you."

Blake's voice was quiet, his tone said something that Jana couldn't quite discern. What she could have told him, what he had to know, was that this would be hard on Lindsey no matter what or when they did it. Time wouldn't make a difference.

"But we're all happy together." Lindsey looked up at him. "Aren't we? And you love my mom."

Lindsey's eyes had filled with tears. Jana reached for her but Lindsey pulled away.

"There's a lot more to a relationship," Blake started and then he shook his head. "I'm sorry, Lindsey."

"You both act like this is just about you. But what about me? You're my mom and dad, and I'm just the kid who doesn't get to make any decisions."

Jana had to step in. "Lindsey, that isn't fair."

"But I thought we'd all be together." She sniffled and wiped her eyes on the back of her arm. "I even thought Teddy and Sissy would be with us. I thought we would all live on the ranch together. I don't want to move anymore."

"You won't." Blake turned a hard look on Jana. "Will you?"

"We're not leaving Dawson. But eventually I do have to get my own place."

"We'll work this out, Lindsey." Blake pulled his daughter close and kissed the top of her head. "I know that isn't what you want to hear, but it's the answer for right now."

Jana didn't know what his answer meant, but it seemed to satisfy Lindsey. They climbed in the truck together and made a quiet trip back to the ranch, with Jana thinking about a man not willing to tell her he loved her and the wall that would always be between them.

The wall had been built by choices she'd made, but she was losing hope that it would fall. She would have lost hope, but then she remembered: even the walls of Jericho fell when God made the plan.

Chapter Thirteen

Blake was up at dawn on Monday morning. He walked through his parents' house, expecting someone to be up. No one was. The house was completely silent, but there were signs of children. A toy truck parked in the living room next to the sofa and a Barbie sitting in a rocking chair. Teddy and Sissy were settling in and making their presence felt. He grinned at that because the two kids seemed to be adjusting. He knew it hadn't been easy at first. There was a lot they couldn't understand.

And there was a lot they weren't going to know about. Not now, with Lisa still missing on the streets of Tulsa. At least they were here and they were safe.

In the kitchen he started a pot of coffee brewing and then sliced himself a piece of apple pie for breakfast. He was munching it down when his dad walked in, still looking half-asleep.

"You're getting around late." Blake nodded toward the pie on the counter.

Tim Cooper took a slice of pie and sat down next to his son. "I'm too old for little ones."

"No, you aren't. You just have to get back in the kid mode. Think how boring this house would be without those two kids."

His dad chewed a bite of pie and then got up for a cup of coffee. He raised the pot, an offer, and Blake nodded. His dad poured two cups and slid them across the counter.

"I was thinking," his dad said as he sat back down, "that you would end up with Teddy and Sissy. Makes more sense to me. You and Teddy have a pretty serious bond."

"I can't imagine them turning two kids over to a single guy living in his parents' guest-house."

His dad took another bite of pie. "Two problems with that statement."

"Great, and I guess you're going to tell me what they are?" He finished his pie and waited.

"Yeah, I am. First, you're not single. Second, you have a house."

"Dad, a month or so back I was as single as any guy around."

"A single guy who hasn't really dated in ten

years means a guy who is still pretty attached to the idea of being married."

"I had other things on my mind. I was looking for my daughter."

"And your wife."

Blake got up to pour himself another cup of coffee. He glanced back at his dad. "I don't recall the search being for Jana."

"I always kind of thought it was."

Blake leaned against the counter holding his cup of coffee, not really interested in drinking it.

"In the sense that she had my daughter, I guess I did search for my wife."

"Why don't you go home?" His dad finished off his pie. "You have a house, a wife and a daughter, and you're living above my garage."

"It isn't that simple. Until last week I thought I was divorced from my wife. And I'm not sure I want to pick up where we left off. I definitely don't want to rush back into a relationship that might fall apart again. What would be harder on Lindsey, us divorcing or the hope that we might work things out only to find that we can't?"

"She made a mistake," Tim admitted.

"Yes, she did."

"I guess we've all made mistakes. And if your mom hadn't been willing to trust me, I probably wouldn't be here. Or she wouldn't."

He was talking about his affair with Jeremy Hightree's mother. An affair that had meant learning that he was Jeremy's dad. It had taken not just their family but the whole community by surprise. It had meant a lot of hurt and anger.

These days, Jeremy was as much a part of the Cooper family as any of them. And Angie Cooper had been his biggest supporter. Blake loved his mom. She was about the most patient, forgiving person in the world. But Blake wasn't his mother.

"I cheated one time, Blake. One mistake and that mistake left ripples. If I had it to do over, I never would have made that choice. But at the same time, I have a son that I love and care about."

"I know you do. Jeremy is my brother. None of us would want to undo that."

"No, but it was wrong, and I'd undo the pain I caused your mother if I could. Give your marriage a chance."

"I'm working on this. I'm struggling with it, though. With trusting her." He returned to his seat next to his dad.

"One day at a time, you let her prove that she's here to stay."

His dad smiled, causing lines around his eyes that had deepened in the past few years. The sun shining through the window caught the gray in his blond hair.

"Remember when you were ten…"

Blake groaned. "Let's not bring that up again."

"Why?"

"Because I'd rather forget."

His dad smiled a gotcha smile. "I'm sure you would."

"I thought I'd smoke one of Uncle Ron's cigars, and I set twenty acres on fire."

"And you never did it again. You didn't smoke again, or play with matches."

"Some people don't learn the first time around. Jackson is a pretty good example of that."

Boots stomped in the direction of the kitchen and Jackson shouted before he came into sight. "Hey, don't use me as an example. I'm living a pretty decent life now. I'm all settled down and respectable."

Blake laughed. "Yeah, you're respectable. Button your shirt."

"I just got up fifteen minutes ago. Give a guy a break." Jackson finished buttoning his shirt and then ran a hand through hair that was standing on end.

"Since when do you sleep in?" Blake shook his head. "Everyone is sleeping in around here."

"I don't get any sleep at night because a little boy is teething."

"That's rough." Blake grinned as he handed Jackson a cup of coffee. He remembered those days, being tired and grouchy. And then missing it like crazy.

He had missed Jana's presence. He'd missed baby stuff all over the house. He'd missed the warmth of his wife and daughter, how it felt to come home to them.

He remembered coming home to an empty house and a note, no little girl running to greet him, no Jana in the kitchen singing off-key to the radio.

"Blake, give it time." His dad stood to leave as he gave that last bit of advice.

"I know."

Jackson took the seat their dad had vacated. "I'm sorry about Jade spilling the beans. She must have overheard us talking, and she thought she was sharing good news. You know how she is about family."

Because she hadn't really had one until she showed up on Jackson's doorstep looking for a dad. Blake got it.

"We're not upset with Jade. We should have told Lindsey."

Jackson shrugged and took a long drink of

coffee. He'd never been bothered by sucking down hot liquid.

"I'm going to move some cattle over to the forty that attaches to your place. Gage got it baled yesterday. Want to ride along?"

That sounded good. He couldn't, though.

"Sounds good but I have to take care of a few things."

"I've got a nice gentle pony you can ride." Jackson laughed as he stood to go.

"I think I'll pass on the pony."

Blake got to his place an hour later. He walked through the front door of the house, rapping once on the frame of the door. It felt strange to knock on the door of the house he had lived in for more than a dozen years.

Music played from the kitchen. He could hear Lindsey talking to Jana. It was no longer baby talk in a toddler voice. Instead it was the voice of a girl who would soon be thirteen. He didn't have any doubts about what she wanted for that birthday.

The house was no longer lifeless, the way it had been since Jana left him. A part of him wanted to keep it this way, with his daughter laughing and Jana singing along to country music.

He walked through the door of the kitchen,

taking off his hat as he went. Jana turned from the sink. She was washing dishes. Lindsey was playing a game on some kind of pocket device he didn't know the name of. They both smiled but he could see hesitancy.

"Do you want coffee?" Jana offered, reaching for a cup. He shook his head.

"You smell like barn," Lindsey informed him and then went back to her game.

"Thanks."

Could a moment get more normal? He thought it couldn't. He smiled at Jana and she looked unsure.

"I have to go to work, but do the two of you want to meet me at the Mad Cow for lunch?" he asked as he stepped back from the sink. "I told Mom I'd pick Teddy up this evening. He's had a rough couple of days, and she thought it might help to spend time with us."

Jana looked from him to Lindsey. Their daughter shrugged a little, and she didn't look as thrilled as he thought she might. Maybe because she was worried. He didn't blame her. She'd had a rough couple of days, too.

He didn't know how to fix it all for her, though. If he thought he could, he would. The only thing he could give her were the normal moments like this one.

* * *

At noon Jana and Lindsey met Blake at the Mad Cow. They were seated in a corner booth, Blake sitting across from them.

"Your birthday is in a couple of weeks." Jana smiled at the waitress who brought their drinks. "Have you thought about what you would like?"

Lindsey was silent for a minute and then she shook her head. "Nothing that I can think of."

"Lindsey..."

Lindsey stopped her. "I don't really want a gift. I can't think of anything I want. But I have been planning my party with Jade and we talked to Granddad. I'll have a slumber party with my cousins. Granddad said we could use the big wagons that they use at Christmas and have a hayride."

"I think that sounds like a great party." Blake leaned back in the seat and smiled at their daughter. "If you want, you can have the slumber party in the stable apartment at Cooper Creek. There's a projector and movie screen stored somewhere if you want to show a movie."

Jana listened to the plans, hoping it would be enough to satisfy their daughter, who really only wanted one thing for her birthday. They all knew, without her saying, that she wanted her parents to reunite.

Jana would love to give her her heart's desire,

but she couldn't. She remembered as a child how she'd wanted to find her birth parents, how it had felt as if her life wouldn't be complete until she knew who they were.

She hadn't realized what it took to be complete. It took faith. It took filling up the emptiness with something outside of herself. She had met her birth parents. They were good people who hadn't thought they could raise a child. They'd hoped she would have love and security with her adoptive parents.

And she had. It had been a different kind of love, nothing at all like the Coopers. It had been quiet, secure. Lindsey felt as if she were missing something. Jana got that.

What she would teach her daughter was that she had two parents who loved her. Two parents who would always be there for her. Even if they couldn't be there for each other.

"Madeline and Jade are here." Blake nodded toward the front door of the café. As if to punctuate the statement, the cowbells hanging over the door clanked together.

Lindsey turned quick, as if she'd already known they would be there. She got up and hurried to Jade's side. The two hugged. Jana loved the sight of her daughter fitting in here. Madeline left the two girls to talk and headed their way.

"We can make room for you," Jana offered.

"We had lunch," Madeline confided. "I'm actually here because our daughters have been texting all morning and they're plotting against us."

"What's the plot?" Blake asked.

Jana scooted and Madeline sat next to her. "I think the plan is for Lindsey to come to our house for a while."

"Oh." Jana turned to look at her daughter, still standing by the counter talking to Jade. "We just ordered."

"We can wait for her food."

Jade and Lindsey returned, both scooting in next to Blake, pushing him up against the wall. Lindsey grinned at her dad and then crossed her arms on the table. "I can get my food to go."

"I don't know." Jana bit down on her lip, not sure about this brave new world that moments ago had seemed so wonderful.

"Mom, I can take my food with me. It'll give you two time to talk adult stuff. Please, for a few hours."

It was the most normal request in the world, and Jana didn't know what to do with it. It had been so long since Lindsey had really been out of her sight. It had been longer since she'd gone home with a friend.

For a year, their lives had been about kidney

disease and hospitals. And she'd dealt with it all alone. She was no longer alone. She looked from her daughter to Blake.

"Did you take your meds before we left?" He moved a little, giving himself more room.

"Yeah. I don't have more until dinner. And I have those in my pack in the car. I always bring it with me just in case we get caught somewhere."

Jana listened and her heart shifted. This was her daughter, growing up, taking responsibility. Becoming independent. When they met with the transplant team each week they discussed these things with Lindsey. Jana had wondered how much a twelve-year-old actually soaked in and how much she ignored. Now she knew. Lindsey was listening.

"I don't see why she can't." Blake looked at Jana for her input.

She hesitated, because it wasn't that easy for her, letting go. Lindsey's eyes widened, waiting.

"You can go."

A few minutes later Vera walked out of the kitchen with a bag and handed it to Lindsey. "There's your salad, kiddo. Ranch on the side."

Blake laughed and Jana felt a little lost.

"How did you know she was leaving?" Jana asked the owner of the Mad Cow, who didn't look at all guilty, but she did give Lindsey a look, brows arched and a smile hovering at the corners of her mouth.

"A little birdy?" Vera quipped.

Jana waited for her daughter to confess, and she did.

"At the register a minute ago. I asked if she would make mine to go. Just in case."

That's how a child turned into a teenager. Jana sat back in her chair and looked at her daughter, the one who had been a little girl not so long ago.

"Fine, go." Jana managed to smile. "And have fun."

Lindsey gave Blake a hug, as if he was the hero she'd been waiting for. Jana let him have the moment. She was going to have to get used to sharing.

The hug she got from her daughter was just as warm, just as tight. Jana hugged her back and held her a moment longer. "Be good."

"Mom!"

And then she was gone, skipping out the door with Madeline and Jade.

Thirty minutes later, Jana and Blake were driving back up to the log home she and Blake had picked together. She remembered that she'd wanted brick, but then he'd taken her to a street in Grove, near Grand Lake and he'd shown her houses like the one he wanted. It seemed to be a trend with these Cooper brothers. Jesse and now Gage also had log-sided homes.

Maybe because they had grown up in the formality of the big brick, Georgian-style home that graced Cooper Creek Ranch? Who had a creek named after them, she wondered? A family that had settled an area long ago, establishing a community and a way of life.

"You're quiet."

She looked at Blake and found a smile. "We have to talk."

"Sounds serious."

"It is, and really, how often do we get to be alone?"

He didn't answer. He pulled up to the garage and parked. "Not often, I guess."

They walked in the front door of the house, greeted by cool air and the smell of roses she'd cut from the flower garden. She'd filled vases with them earlier, and the scent hung in the air.

"The house looks good." Blake walked with her to the kitchen. "It feels like a home again."

"I don't know what to say to that." She poured herself a glass of water.

"The house was empty for a long time. Just one man rattling around in this place doesn't make it a home."

"I know."

As they walked to the kitchen, she heard the

familiar scratching at the back door. She hoped Blake wouldn't hear. He did. He went to the utility room and looked out.

"Why is my dog at the back door, acting like this is the way he gets let inside?"

She smiled and opened the door. "Because it is."

"He's a farm dog. What have you done to him?"

Sam ran to the area in the utility room where she'd placed food and water bowls for him. His tail wagged, and he looked back at Blake, just momentarily.

"It's really hot outside," Jana explained. "He has all of that thick, long fur."

"Right, and plenty of shade and a pond to swim in."

"He makes me feel safe at night."

He laughed at that. "You think that dog is going to protect you? He's the biggest chicken around."

"He's not. He's very brave." She said it in a voice that made Sam thump his tail a little more.

Blake shook his head and walked off. "I've lost. My house smells like roses and there's a dog sleeping in my bed. With my wife."

"Am I your wife, Blake?" She followed him into the kitchen. "Because it doesn't feel like it. It feels like I'm a temporary guest in your home."

Blake walked to the French doors that led to the patio. He glanced back at her only briefly. "I'm not sure who you are or who we are."

She changed the subject. "How are Teddy and Sissy doing? Any news on their mother?"

"No, she's still missing. They think she's probably on the streets. Her family said that she went through this years ago, before the children. She was on the streets quite a while before she got help."

"It happens to people every day. I was fortunate that I got help and I had the resources to keep up my medical care. I was fortunate that my depression wasn't chronic."

"I'm just not sure what will happen to the kids." Blake sat down at the dining room table.

Jana stood at the door, unable to sit. "You should have had more children. You should have had a son."

"We can't go back, Jana."

"No, we can't. But I need for you to know this."

He rested folded hands on the table. "I'm not sure if I like the way this sounds."

"I'm not leaving, if that's what you think." She looked away, because it was hard to talk with his hazel eyes watching her, intense, questioning.

"Okay, then what are we talking about?"

"I'm not leaving." She started again. The dog had wandered in from the utility room, and he sat down at her feet, looking up with dark eyes that always seemed to understand.

"Jana?" Blake's voice was soft, but she knew he was losing patience.

"I'm moving to town. I can't stay here. I think if I stay here, it gives Lindsey the wrong ideas about us. She's holding on to hope that we're going to be a family again."

Maybe Jana had been holding on to the same hope. Hope had been vanquished when a few days earlier she had answered the phone and it had been the lawyer handling the divorce, wanting to confirm an appointment. She'd given him Blake's cell number.

He didn't answer. He stood and walked to the French door. The dog moved to his side, and he reached down to run his hand across Sam's head. The dog whimpered softly. Blake turned around, his eyes dark and unreadable.

"Where are you going to live?"

"Mia's house, believe it or not. With Breezy." She and Mia's half sister had become friends because they both felt somewhat out of place in Dawson.

"I'm really not sure why you think this is necessary."

"Aren't you, Blake? This is your house. You've

mentioned that a time or two. You've moved out, and you're living in a guesthouse at Cooper Creek. It's all temporary. Lindsey and I living here, you living there. All temporary. It's as if our lives are on hold. We need something permanent. Lindsey needs to know that her parents are here for her, but that maybe we can't give her what she wants."

Blake walked away. She followed him to the living room, and she waited for him to say something. She wanted him to disagree and tell her she was wrong. She wanted him to get mad and say something that would make sense and put an end to this. She couldn't live in limbo this way.

And yet, his life had been in limbo for ten years. She'd been the cause. Maybe it was her turn to wait for him.

"Blake, please. Say something."

He brushed a hand through his hair and sank onto the sofa, his face in his hands. "I want you here. I want you in my life. And at the same time, I'm not sure how to give you a second chance. Every single time I come over here, I worry that you're not going to be here."

She sat down next to him. "That's the problem, Blake. I'm not a twenty-four-year-old woman anymore, uncomfortable in my own skin and trying to figure out the darkness by myself."

He sat back on the sofa and she settled next to him.

"Jana, I can't tell you that I'm ready to call off the divorce. I want to. I want to move back in here and take up where we left off, like none of it ever happened. But it did happen. And what if we, the people we are now, don't work as a couple? Then we've given Lindsey false hope."

"So, I move to town and you get back to your life." And maybe someday, she thought. Maybe he would work through this and trust her again.

"I wish the two of you would stay here."

"I can't. The longer I stay, the more Lindsey gets attached to the idea of the three of us in this house. She needs to realize that if things don't work out between us, she's not going to lose either of her parents. I want her settled somewhere."

"Right, I get it." He stood and walked to the front door. "I have to get back to work."

"Blake, I'm sorry."

He nodded, his hand on the doorknob. "I'll be back tonight so we can tell Lindsey. I won't bring Teddy, not tonight."

"We'll be here."

"When are you going to leave?"

She put a hand over his. "I'm not leaving, I'm moving to our own place."

"Okay, when are you moving?"

"In a few days."

He kissed her goodbye. It took her by surprise the way his lips claimed hers. She moved her hand to his shoulder and closed her eyes, wishing she could stay in his arms forever. She didn't want to walk away from him, not even temporarily.

Chapter Fourteen

Blake showed up at six to have dinner with Jana and Lindsey. He'd left Teddy and Sissy with his parents. Tonight he had to sit down with his daughter and tell her she was moving out of the house she'd come to see as her home. It didn't sit well with him, but he could see Jana's side of things.

They needed time. *He* needed time.

When he got to the front porch, Lindsey was there waiting. She opened the door and gave him a narrow-eyed look, stepping back to let him inside.

"Mom said we have to talk."

"Hi to you, too." He took off his hat and hung it on the hook by the door. "Where is your mom?"

"Getting ready. I don't know why, if we're

staying home. She made chicken casserole and some kind of strange pie she said you like."

"What kind is that?"

"Gooseberry?"

"One of my favorites."

"I tried one—they're gross. I'll stick to cinnamon rolls." She made a face to go with the statement. "Is this about you guys being married?"

"Yeah, it is."

He followed her to the kitchen. She picked up a cinnamon roll and took a bite, licking frosting off her fingers. He watched her for a minute, because she was his kid and she was back. Jana was back. He couldn't untangle the feelings. He had ten years of being angry and a month of being relieved and some other crazy emotions that had to do with Jana.

"You could just tell her you love her and then we could be a family."

Blake didn't know what to say to that. "Lindsey, life is a little more complicated than that."

"You could just move back in," Lindsey tried, looking up at him with her pixie face framed by dark hair.

"It isn't that simple."

"Yes, it is. You adults make everything more complicated than it has to be. You're my parents and you're still married."

He shook his head. "We are the adults and

we have to make this decision, Lindsey. I know you want us to be together, the three of us, but we have to be able to make a marriage work."

"It could be the five of us."

She was including Sissy and Teddy. He smiled at that, because who wouldn't want those two included in a family plan. If, he thought, if Jana hadn't left, maybe they would have been a family of five by now. Lindsey would have had younger brothers and sisters.

"You could at least think about it." Lindsey smiled as she said it. She scooped a cinnamon roll out of the pan and put it on a plate, sliding it in front of him.

"I'll take that under consideration. I thought there was gooseberry pie?" He followed her to the table.

She took another bite of her cinnamon roll. "Who wants gooseberry if you can have cinnamon?"

He laughed at that. "People who like gooseberry? And aren't we having chicken casserole?"

Shoes clicked on the tile floor. He turned, and for a long moment he was lost in time, in some place that made everything else fade away. Jana stood there, unsure but beautiful. The sundress she wore flowed, but swirled around her legs. Her eyes were vivid blue and her blond hair framed her face. They weren't kids anymore, but man, she was still as beautiful as ever.

"Nice dress." He choked the words out. Next to him, Lindsey laughed.

"Nice dress?" his daughter questioned. "You can't do better than that?"

"Hot." He reached for the cup of coffee Lindsey had poured before he sat down. "The coffee is hot."

Jana turned pink and pretended she hadn't gotten it. "I need a cup of coffee, too."

"The cinnamon rolls are good."

"We're having chicken casserole for dinner." She poured herself a cup of coffee. "You'll ruin your appetite."

"Too late. And Lindsey said you have gooseberry pie?"

"For dessert."

Blake stood and pulled a chair out for Jana. She sat down, smiling up at him.

And then her smile dissolved, because he was there for a reason and not a pleasant one. Lindsey looked first at him and then at Jana. Her smile had disappeared, and she bit down on her bottom lip.

"You're going to give me bad news."

"Not really," Jana started. She looked to him and he shook his head. This was her game plan, not his.

"Lindsey, I've made a decision…"

Before she could explain, Lindsey stood and backed away, her eyes wide. "I'm not going anywhere. You can't make me."

"I'm not." Jana stood and went to their daughter, pulling her into a hug that Lindsey pulled away from. "We're not leaving Dawson."

"But?" Lindsey moved away from her mother, closer to Blake's side. The look in her eyes broke his heart, but he reminded himself that Jana had her reasons for doing this. She had good reasons, he guessed.

He could stop her, he realized as she stood there trying to find words to tell her daughter they were moving out of this house. A part of him wanted to stop her. For Lindsey's sake. And he realized it had to be for more than his daughter's sake.

Maybe it was and he just wasn't ready.

"Lindsey, listen to your mom," he broke in, giving her a look that he hoped said they would get through this.

She sat back down, but her gaze lowered to her hands in her lap. "Okay, I'm listening."

"We're moving to Dawson," Jana explained. "We're going to live with Breezy for a while."

"Why?"

"Because I want your dad to have his home and his life back."

"We're here, though, and he's my dad and you're his wife."

"Right, you are his daughter, but the other, Lindsey, that's something we have to work through. If that paperwork wouldn't have been misfiled, we would have been divorced. Because of a clerical error we're not."

"Lindsey, there are things your mom and I have to figure out for ourselves. These decisions take time. But this is still your home. You can come here whenever you want."

"So you could decide to stay together." Looking from him to her mom, she smiled, then frowned. "Or you could decide to not stay together."

"Right, those are our choices." It sounded harsh even to him, but she needed to know the truth.

Not the whole truth, he thought. Not the part where he wondered if his wife wanted to be married to him. She'd come home for Lindsey's sake, not for a reunion with her husband.

"Okay."

That was it. *Okay.* She got up and walked to the kitchen. Jana smiled at him and followed their daughter. He wanted to give Lindsey everything. But he couldn't make promises that they might not be able to keep. He and Jana would make sure she had two parents in her life, loving her. He could promise Lindsey they would be together.

Two days later, Jana decided it was time to pack their meager belongings and leave. Blake had been around but he had remained distant. That wasn't what she wanted. She had thought they could work on deciding what they wanted from this marriage they still found themselves in.

Instead Blake withdrew. Not from Lindsey, but from her. That wasn't what Jana wanted.

She wanted Blake Cooper as her husband.

All of the things she'd run from, thinking they would suffocate her, were now the things she wanted most in her life...and the things that were the furthest from her grasp.

As she packed, she thought about leaving their home a second time. The last time it had been an escape. This time? She was giving Blake back his home. She was giving him space and time.

Lindsey wasn't happy. Jana liked to think that someday her daughter would understand, but she didn't know if Lindsey would. To Lindsey, there were simple black-and-white choices in life, and she couldn't understand a decision like this one.

Lindsey walked in and sat down on the bedroom floor. "Do we have to do this?"

Jana folded clothes and put them in her suitcase. "Yes."

"For how long?"

How long would she wait? She'd been asking herself that question for a while and she knew the answer. She would wait as long as it took. She didn't want anyone else. She only wanted Blake Cooper.

"Mom?"

She looked up, smiling at her daughter. "I'm not sure how long, Linds. Your dad and I need to know what we feel for each other. We don't want to make a mistake and have you hurt again."

"Yeah, I get that."

"I know this is hard, but you'll see. Things will work out. We've always managed, haven't we?"

"Yeah, but I just thought…" Lindsey looked away. She brushed at her cheeks and sniffled. "I thought God would answer my prayers."

Jana let out a breath. She didn't want this for her daughter, this doubt, this pain. "Honey, God hears you. I don't think the problem is God's ability to answer prayers. It's our ability to hear His answers."

"Yeah, well, get your hearing checked." Lindsey drew her knees up to her chest and hugged them tight, resting her head there the way she'd done when she was little and upset. Or not getting her way.

"We'll try, Lindsey. But no matter what, we'll be fine. Your dad is here and I'm here."

Jana hadn't expected those words to hurt, but they did. She kept thinking of that call from the lawyer, knowing that Blake had called them about the divorce before talking it over with her. And it hurt.

It hurt worse than coming home and wondering what would happen when she reappeared in his life.

Lindsey looked up. "What about Sam?"

"He's a farm dog—he can't come with us."

Lindsey's head sank again. "I have my bags packed," she mumbled into her knees.

Jana moved to her daughter's side and wrapped her in a hug. "I'm listening to God, Lindsey. I know that doesn't make sense because it hurts, but I am listening. Your dad needs his home back. He needs time and space to decide what he wants."

Lindsey shook her head and looked up. "You don't get to decide if you want your kid."

"I didn't mean he's deciding *if* he wants you. Of course he wants you. He loves you."

Lindsey's face scrunched in thought. "Are

you saying you think he doesn't want you? That's crazy, Mom. He loves you."

"Maybe he does, but maybe he hasn't figured it out yet."

"Because he's been mad at you a long time?"

"Yeah."

Jana leaned back against her bed, pulling Lindsey with her. The two of them sat there a long time with Jana wishing she didn't have to pack. She kept waiting, hoping she would hear Blake pull up. She kept praying he would rush in and tell them not to go.

Today was the day Blake's lawyer had confirmed that they had an afternoon appointment to discuss the divorce.

She couldn't spend her life waiting for Blake, wondering if each day would be the day he showed up to tell them their marriage was over.

Chapter Fifteen

Blake walked into an empty house. No hint of rose perfume in the air, no music played from the kitchen, no youth-size boots at the front door. No Lindsey running to greet him. And no Jana smiling to welcome him back. He had never wanted to replay that moment when they'd disappeared, leaving him with an empty home and a shell of a life for ten years.

The last time Jana left, Lindsey had been two. Now she was almost thirteen. Her birthday was less than a week away. They had plans for a slumber party and a wagon ride around Cooper Creek. Lindsey's cousins and a few friends from church would be there.

Once again he was starting over alone. Because Jana thought he needed his house and his life back. He threw his hat on the couch and stomped through the living room. The basic need to throw something overtook him, but there wasn't anything within reach to throw and nothing he really wanted to break.

When he got to the kitchen he stopped short. There was a note on the counter. He picked it up, shaken by the memory of finding that note years ago, the one that told him he no longer had a wife and daughter.

This time the note was from Lindsey.

He sat down at the island and held it in his hands, wishing he could hold on to that old stereotype that men don't cry. Because when men are confronted with a note from their daughter in an empty house, an empty life, they cry.

Daddy, I love you and I'm so glad you'll always be a part of me. For real, because I have your kidney. No matter where we go or what happens, you'll always be with me. But we're not gone, we're just in Dawson and I want to come out and stay with you. So please, forgive my mom. She loves you.

It wasn't possible to rip a person's heart out, not literally, but that letter nearly did him in. He sat there for a long time, until late-afternoon shadows drifted across the kitchen. Outside, the dog barked and then scratched at the door. He didn't get up.

They had moved to town three days ago. It had taken him this long to walk back in the house. He didn't want this life back. He didn't want this empty house.

Jana didn't get that. She'd told him she needed to figure out what her life in Dawson would be. Because she couldn't live in his home in some kind of crazy holding pattern, wondering what would happen between the two of them.

His feelings were like a ball of string that someone had wadded up. He was unraveling, trying to figure out what he felt.

Someone banged on the front door. He didn't answer it. A few minutes later he heard heavy footsteps in the living room. Jackson shouted his name, asking where he was hiding. Blake folded the note and shoved it in his pocket.

"I'm in here."

Jackson walked through the door, shaking his head the way he did when he thought something was ridiculous. "Sitting in the dark feeling sorry for yourself? That isn't the way I've always pictured my older brother. Is that what you've done in this house all these years?"

"No, it isn't. And I've got work to do."

"Yeah, you have work to do." Jackson walked into the kitchen and helped himself to the coffeemaker, filling the water reservoir and pushing the power button. "The least you could do is offer a man a cup of coffee that isn't girlie."

Jackson sifted through the pods in the rack next to the coffeemaker. "Hazelnut? French vanilla? Do you have any normal coffee? It's almost like a woman has been living here."

Jackson grinned as he pushed his hat back and gave Blake a long look.

"What are you doing here?"

"Checking on you. It would seem people are a little worried."

"There's no reason to be worried."

Jackson snorted. "Of course not. So where's some good, strong, rip-your-insides-out-and-keep-you-up-all-night kind of coffee?"

"I think in the cabinet."

"That's what happens when you have a wife. They put away all the man stuff and replace it with girl stuff."

"I don't have a wife."

"Actually, you do. That's what I'm here to talk about. You have a wife and a daughter. And your stubborn hide, after ten years of searching, let them walk back out of your life."

"It isn't crazy from where I'm sitting. Jana..."

"Yeah, whatever." Jackson brewed himself a cup of coffee and stood in the kitchen drinking it. "I have a trailer full of cattle in my truck that I need to get home."

"You bought more?"

"Good heifers. A farmer in Missouri was selling out, turning his farm into a subdivision." Jackson shook his head.

"Do you need help unloading them?"

Jackson crossed his arms over his chest. "Yeah, because I can't unload cattle."

"I know you can."

"Come with me, then. Madeline put a roast on this morning. There will be plenty for you, since you don't have anyone here to eat with."

Blake had started to stand but changed his mind. "I've had about all of your brotherly support I can handle for one day."

Jackson laughed as he pounded Blake on the back and walked out of the kitchen. "Suit yourself."

He waited until he heard Jackson's truck and the creaking of the stock trailer as it went down the drive and then he got up and headed for the front door. He had animals to feed and a dog that needed attention. Sam was waiting for him at the front door.

Blake ruffled his hand through the dog's fur. "It's just you and me, Sam."

The dog trotted off ahead of him in search of a stick.

Blake was in the field watching a cow that looked like she might drop her calf anytime.

The last time she'd calved he had to pull the calf. He was hoping this time wouldn't be a repeat. His phone buzzed in his pocket, and he pulled it out to answer it.

"Jana."

"Blake, is Lindsey out there?"

The question brought his heart to a stop. He walked away, forgetting the cow, forgetting everything.

"No, she isn't. Why?"

"She went for a walk and didn't come back. It's been over an hour. I've driven around town and can't find her anywhere."

"I'll check the house and then I'll head that way."

"Blake, I'm scared."

He started to tell her not to be, but since his insides were shaking, he couldn't. "Yeah, me, too."

A minute later he was in his truck, Sam in the seat next to him. The dog had insisted. Funny how animals could do that; they just seemed to know when something was wrong with their people.

Where could Lindsey be? Blake tried to think the way a twelve-year-old would think. What would make her take off? And had she taken off? What if someone…

He shook his head, not wanting to let his

mind dwell on that thought. As he drove, he called Slade. His brother-in-law was a police officer and would get this search moving in the right direction.

When Slade answered, Blake broke right in to the conversation. "We can't find Lindsey. Or Jana can't find her. She went for a walk."

"I know. Jana called. I put it out on the radio and we have everyone looking—local, county and state. We'll find her."

"Thank you. I'm on my way to town right now."

"Did you check to make sure she wasn't at your place?"

Blake glanced in his rearview mirror; the house was out of sight. "I was just there."

"Go get Jana and then make another check of your place. We don't want to search the whole countryside and then find her sitting in her bedroom at your place."

"Good point."

Get Jana. He realized that as soon as she called, his natural reaction had been to get to her side. He'd done that years ago when she'd gone into labor. He'd done it when Lindsey cut her finger when she was a toddler. Get to Jana, make her world right.

It didn't bother him, life repeating itself. He pulled his truck into the driveway of Mia's old house. Jana came out the front door, tears streaming down her cheeks. He got out and waited for her, knowing. She would need him.

She fell into his arms, holding on for what felt like dear life. He held her, promising they would find their daughter.

They had to find her. The idea of not finding her became a white-hot pain in his chest, taking hold of his brain, making him forget what they needed to do. He had to get control, at least of himself.

"Did she say anything at all? Anything that would give a hint to what she was thinking? How was she acting?"

Jana shook her head against his chest. "I don't know."

"Jana, you have to get it together and help me."

She pulled back, wiping her eyes. "I know."

"Okay."

She took a deep breath, closing her eyes as a few more tears trickled down her cheeks. "What if someone took her?"

"We'll find her."

"It's my fault. I thought we needed to give you space and let you have your place back. I didn't realize how much it would hurt her. I always mess up and hurt the people I love."

"Jana, not now. Let's concentrate on Lindsey. Did she say anything at all?"

Jana shook her head. "Not really. She grabbed her music and went out the door. She said she needed to get fresh air."

"Then we'll find her. She's being a typical, upset teenager. She's hiding somewhere, being mad at us." A little bit of calm returned as he put the pieces together.

They would find their daughter. And when they did, they had to sit down and discuss their lives, because he couldn't keep Jana and Lindsey in turmoil, in limbo.

It was time to untangle their lives and see what they had left.

Jana climbed in the truck, thankful for a place to sit down. Her legs trembled and she hugged herself tight. Sam the dog moved against her, his face close to hers. Blake told him to lie down and he did, with his head on her lap.

"She isn't a typical teenager, Blake. I know that's what she wants to be, but she isn't. She didn't take her medication with her. What if something happens and she gets hurt?"

Blake pulled the truck onto the road and shot her a look that told her to stop. It was a pretty obvious look, she thought.

"Jana, you have to stop making her feel different. We all know she has challenges. We know her life isn't typical. But she is a typical teenager, and you have to let her be one, as much as you possibly can."

"You're saying I made her run?"

He smiled an easy smile. "I'm not saying you made her run. Our situation made her take off. That's the typical teen part. You have to accept that even with her health issues, she's still an almost-thirteen-year-old girl."

"Right, of course." Her hands shook. She clasped them together and watched out the window. Blake touched her arm, and she reached, letting him take her hand.

"She'll be fine." His assurance slipped over her like calming waters. Peace. She'd been praying since she realized Lindsey hadn't come back from her walk.

"I know. But where is she?"

"She's somewhere close. She gets tired easily. She'll be somewhere close."

Jana watched him, knowing that he was thinking. He was being the analytical Blake, the man who took things apart and studied each individual piece. He'd probably done that with their relationship, too.

It wasn't long before they were pulling up to Blake's house. Her house, too. She kept thinking of it as Blake's, but her heart was in this house.

She loved it. She felt more at home there than anywhere else.

"We'll check the barn and the animals first. She loves being out here with the animals." Blake stopped the truck. "I'll check the equipment shed and around the yard.

Jana jumped down from the truck, the dog following, and headed for the barn. She went stall to stall, looking inside each one. She looked in the tack room. She walked through the back door of the barn into the field where cattle grazed. Next, she walked to the small paddock where he kept the pony, because the grass was green and he worried the smaller animal would eat too much and founder. The pony raised his shaggy head but went back to munching grass.

"Lindsey?" She cupped her hands to her mouth and called out, wanting a response, hoping for one and knowing deep down that she wouldn't get one.

As she walked toward the house, she tried Lindsey's phone again. No reply. Of course she didn't answer. If she was hiding or had run away, she obviously didn't want to be found.

Jana made a quick search of the house and then walked back outside. Blake was still somewhere searching. She stood on the front porch and scanned the field. The dog roamed the yard, nose to the ground as if he too was looking for Lindsey.

When Blake walked up the steps a few minutes later, she lost the thin thread of control she'd been holding on to. She thought about all the times over the years when he hadn't been there and she'd wanted him at her side. The times she'd missed him because she didn't have his strong arms to turn to.

She had missed him every single day. Had she told him that?

"We're going to find her." He reached for her hand.

She nodded and leaned into his side as they crossed the yard to the truck. "I'm so sorry, Blake."

"You didn't do anything."

"I'm sorry I hurt you. And I wanted you to know, I missed you every single day I was gone. I missed you."

"Let's find our daughter, and we'll talk about this later."

He opened the door for her and she climbed in. The dog jumped in next, getting in the middle again as Blake got behind the wheel.

"This is how it felt, isn't it?" Jana sighed and reached for his hand because she suddenly got it. She knew what he'd gone through.

"What?"

"This is how it felt when you didn't know where we were. When you were searching for us." She shook her head. "For Lindsey, not for me."

She'd thought about that a lot lately, and it had hurt, even though she got it. She understood why the focus of his search would have been for their daughter and not the wife who had taken her.

But that didn't mean she didn't hurt over it. She wanted him to want her back, not just Lindsey. He had to want them both or they couldn't be a family.

Chapter Sixteen

He hadn't expected it to be a day of revelations. He wanted to find his daughter, not delve too deeply into what made up his relationship with his wife. He'd been doing enough of that lately. But there was a look in Jana's eyes, a pain he couldn't deny.

Strings were unraveling. He was sorting things out.

"You were the one who left, Jana. I thought you wanted to be out of my life. I guess I didn't think finding you would do any good because you knew how to come home if you wanted to."

"I didn't, not really." Something in her blue eyes pleaded for understanding. "I didn't know how to explain things or what your reaction would be. I knew the way home, but I didn't know how to get here."

Why did that put him in mind of so many

people in the world? Runaways from life, the homeless, the lost. They knew the way home but didn't know how to get back. People wanted to go home but didn't know if they'd be accepted once they got there.

Teddy's mom was one of those people.

His wife had been one of those runaways. *His wife.*

He pulled the truck onto the highway, needing the search to keep his mind busy.

"I didn't just come home for Lindsey." Jana's comment took him back to their conversation.

"Not now, Jana." He turned down a side road and refocused on the search. "We need to find Lindsey. Did she take anything with her?"

"She had her backpack, and when I asked why, she said she had a granola bar and a bottle of water. I should have been thinking and known she might do this."

That information helped him breathe a little easier, but not a lot. He wouldn't take a good deep breath until they had her safe with them.

"You called Jade, right?"

Jana nodded, but her focus remained on the road. He couldn't see her face, her expression. He knew that she was probably crying.

"I called Sabrina, too. Just in case. They aren't as close, but I thought she might have called."

"We're going to find her. Someone will see

her." He offered the reassurance, needing to believe it himself.

"I know." Jana shifted in the seat, giving him a sweet glimpse of her profile. "But that isn't going to solve the problem. The problem is us. We caused her to do this."

He had another theory. "Or she's desperate and pulling one last Granny Myrna stunt."

"Stunt?" She looked a little outraged by his use of the word.

"Trying to push us together."

Her mouth shaped an O. "She wouldn't."

He laughed at that. "Of course she would. She's a Cooper. We always get what we want."

"What do you want, Blake?"

He couldn't answer that right now, not when he was starting to see things more clearly. He still had a lot to process.

"Let's just find Lindsey."

He drove the back way to Dawson, slowly, letting cars pass as they came up behind him. Almost to town, Slade pulled up next to him in a patrol car. The driver's side window rolled down. Blake shifted into Park and the two of them sat there on that country road with the sun setting and the sky in shades of blue and pink.

"No luck." Slade pushed back his hat and craned his neck to look up at Blake in the truck. "Mia wants you to call her."

"I will."

"She said it's pretty important."

"Okay. I'll go by your place." Blake shifted back into Drive, his foot still on the brake. "I just don't have a clue where she would have gone to."

"Me neither, but I'd say she's closer than we think."

They drove on toward town. Blake slowed as they went past the Mad Cow. "Are you hungry?"

"I couldn't eat. But if you want something…"

He shook his head. "I'm not hungry."

A few minutes later, they pulled up at Mia and Slade's little ranch-style house. Mia walked out the front door with some kind of electronic contraption in her hand. She had a big smile on her face.

"What's up?" Blake got out of the truck. He and Jana met Mia on the front steps of her house.

"I know where she is." Mia held out the gizmo in her hand.

"How do you know where she is?" Jana peeked at the thing, and Blake held it out to her. It was a screen with a bright blue dot on a map.

He had forgotten. Even when Jana had mentioned the music Lindsey had taken with her, it hadn't registered. Now, looking at Mia's happy smile and the gizmo in her hand, he remembered, and he could have hugged his little sister for her suspicious nature.

Unfortunately Jana was looking from Mia to him, and she didn't look at all happy. He guessed he wouldn't, either.

"Explain it, Mia." Blake headed for his truck with the two women trailing behind. "And tell me where I need to go."

"Head back to town." Mia opened the passenger side door, and Jana climbed in ahead of her, pushing the console back to make a middle seat.

"How do you know where my daughter is, Mia?" Jana didn't sound at all pleased.

Blake grinned, feeling relieved enough to be a little bit happy with his sister.

Mia cleared her throat, once, then twice. She looked more than a little guilty. "When you first got back to town, I wasn't convinced you would stay. I was worried you would take Lindsey and leave again."

Mia held up her electronic gizmo.

"So you planted something on my daughter?" Jana looked pretty outraged. Her normally soft tones raised a couple of levels and her cheeks were pink.

"Yes, it's in the MP3 player. I'm really sorry. I just thought…"

"You thought I would leave." Jana spoke in a quieter voice.

"Yes, I thought you would leave. And I wanted to know that we could find Lindsey."

"I'm not leaving." Jana didn't look at either of them. "I'm really very tired of trying to convince Blake, and the people in his life, that I'm here to stay."

"I know." Mia patted her arm. "I'm sorry."

Jana nodded.

"Can you tell me where we're going?" Blake asked, shooting his sister a look. He tried not to look too closely at Jana. She was hurt. They would have to work through that later.

Mia brought the screen down to a smaller scale. Blake put his focus back on the road.

"She's at the rodeo grounds."

Blake turned the truck around in the middle of the road and headed back toward Dawson and the rodeo grounds at the edge of town.

He knew the coming hours, even days, would be spent dealing with his life, his family. But first, he was getting his daughter back.

The truck flew down the road a little faster than Jana would have preferred. Mia was on the phone calling Slade, and then she called Angie and Tim, because she knew they'd been searching, too.

This was how it felt to be loved, to have family. The realization took deep root in Jana's heart, because it was this love and support that she'd run from, that she'd taken her daughter from. She'd been so foolish.

She couldn't even be mad at Mia for not trusting her. They had every reason to suspect that she would leave again.

They stopped next to the bleachers of the arena. Jana saw her daughter immediately. She practically scrambled over Mia to get out. As she ran the short distance, Lindsey looked up, actually appearing surprised.

"Mom?"

"Where have you been?"

Lindsey looked around, blinking a few times. "I've been here. It's peaceful. Is everything okay?"

Jana sat down next to Lindsey. "Honey, we were worried. We thought…"

Lindsey's eyes widened. "You thought I ran away."

"You were gone a long time. I tried to call your cell phone."

"It's in my bag. I was listening to music and then I decided to just sit here for a while and watch the sunset. The sky was pink and the trees were dark green and there were lightning bugs."

"Oh, Lindsey."

"I'm really sorry. I didn't mean to worry everyone."

"Next time, maybe you could watch the time and call to let us know where you are?" Blake had joined them. He sat on the other side of his daughter. "I called to let everyone know you're safe."

Jana reached for Lindsey's hand. "Maybe we should go."

"How'd you find me?" Lindsey asked as they walked down off the bleachers.

"That would be thanks to your aunt Mia," Blake answered as they headed for the truck where Mia was waiting.

"She knew where I was?" Lindsey dropped her MP3 player in her backpack.

"She might have had a clue." Jana smiled, unwilling to tell her daughter the truth.

They took Mia home and then went back to the house in town. Breezy had gone to work, but she'd left a salad and homemade ranch dressing on the table. Lindsey went to her room, exhausted from her walk and promising to eat later.

Jana stood in the bright little kitchen that had once been Mia's. She turned to look at her ex-husband. "I'm sorry for today, for all the drama."

"It isn't your fault, or even Lindsey's. She

should have called, but she didn't know we'd all panic."

"No, she didn't."

He tossed his hat on the counter and walked toward her. She waited, wanting to be held, wanting his lips on hers. But he stopped. It was as if a wall had suddenly been erected between them.

"I need to go." He swept a hand through his hair, and she could see him struggling, see it in his eyes, in the line of his jaw.

"There's plenty of salad," she offered.

"No, I have to go. I can't think straight when I'm around you."

"Why do you always have to think straight, think everything through? Can't you just feel, Blake? Can't you hold me and know that we could be good again."

"I wish I was that guy, the guy who just let go and gave in, Jana. I'm not. I never have been." He reached for his hat. "That's wrong. I was once. The day I met you, I was that guy. But I'm knocking on the door of forty and life has taught me a lot."

She wouldn't beg him to stay.

In the end he stepped close, leaning to place an easy kiss on her forehead. She heard the release of his breath, felt the tenseness in his touch as his hand brushed her back in a soft hug.

"I'll see you in a day or two. We need to finish planning Lindsey's birthday party."

She nodded as tears filled her eyes and Blake walked away.

Chapter Seventeen

The birthday party was in full swing. Blake watched his daughter in the center of a group of family and friends. They were ready for the wagon ride and bonfire. Perfect timing. The sun was setting, and it would be down to eighty-five degrees soon. This time of year that was almost a cold front. Or at least that's what the forecasters called it.

"Roasting hot dogs and marshmallows on a day that the thermometer on my porch hit nearly a hundred degrees." Jackson had walked up, and to illustrate the heat he took off his hat and swiped an arm across his forehead.

Blake had to grin. "For the first time in a long time, I don't care how hot it is. It isn't too hot for this bonfire."

"No, I guess not."

Blake watched the girls gather in a big group,

all smiles in anticipation of the bonfire, the ice cream his mom had made and music with Gage.

"It's been a good day," Jackson admitted. "I kind of wish I'd worn shorts, though."

"You, in shorts?" Blake would have to see it.

"I own a few pairs."

"Only because Madeline dresses you now."

"Yeah, well, it wouldn't hurt you to have a little help in that department."

"Don't interfere," Blake warned. "I'm having a good day, sharing my daughter's birthday."

"I know."

His first birthday with her in eleven years. He was loving every minute of it. He had seen the cake. He had bought gifts she would actually open, not the ones that were stacked in the attic. Presents he'd never given her. He'd thought about giving them to her and decided against it. He was letting go of the past, not dragging it out of the attic and presenting it to his daughter so that she too could hold on to it.

Letting go hadn't been easy. Ten years of bottled-up resentment wasn't something a man just let go of. But understanding helped.

Jackson said something and walked away. Blake watched his younger brother as he found his wife, hugged her tight and kissed her like no one was watching. Blake felt a strong tug of envy.

"Can I ride next to you?" Jana somehow had come to stand next to him. He had seen her only twice since the false alarm of Lindsey running away. He'd spent a hard week getting his thoughts in order, dealing with the past and with the junk in his life that had kept him tied up in knots.

He'd spent a lot of time planning a sweet-thirteen party that his daughter would never forget. He smiled because he knew it would be everything she wanted from a party.

"You sure can." He nodded toward the wagon. "Get aboard."

He watched with a growing smile, appreciating the view as Jana put a foot on the tiny step and hauled herself into the seat.

When she turned, he swallowed the goofy grin he knew she'd see on his face, and he reached to pull himself up. The girls were climbing in the back of the wagon. The rest of his family had opted to walk or ride in one of the farm trucks. His parents, a couple of brothers, sisters and all of their spouses—everyone was there. They wouldn't miss this party for anything. What had started as a birthday party for his daughter had turned into something of a reunion, a welcome home party.

The girls were all in the back of the wagon, and Gage and his wife, Layla, rode with them, teaching them campfire songs. Gage was playing his old acoustic guitar. The voices of the girls were loud and laced with laughter. Man, this was the life. This was his life.

He planned on holding on to it. He glanced back, watching the girls as they looped arms in the back of the wagon and sang silly songs with Gage. Teddy and Sissy were in the middle, close to Lindsey.

Blake had spent a day searching Tulsa, trying to bring their mother home. He'd tried homeless shelters, because that's where people often ended up when they couldn't find their way home. People like Lisa, who were struggling, sometimes off medication and unable to call home. He'd searched the streets and passed around pictures of her.

It hurt that he couldn't find her for them.

"This is perfect, isn't it?" Jana kept her distance, sitting on the far edge of the seat. "It isn't as hot as they had forecasted."

"It's pretty close to perfect. It will be about five degrees cooler down by the creek."

The creek was in sight. Lucky's truck was already there. He and Travis had the fire going, and it was a doozy. Blake pulled the team up a good distance away, giving the horses a break from the bright blaze and the heat. The girls in the back of the wagon all piled out.

Blake's parents were in charge, handing out roasting sticks, hot dogs and then stationing girls around the fire. There was a table set up with all the fixings. The sun was going down behind the trees, leaving the valley a cool place, dark green, tree frogs and birds singing in the trees and the occasional splash of a fish jumping in the creek.

Jana walked among the girls, talking, laughing. Blake watched her, and he wouldn't let himself wish for the ten years that were gone—years he couldn't get back. She smiled at their daughter. The two looked a lot alike, even though Jana was fair and Lindsey had his dark hair. They laughed together, and Lindsey stuck a hot dog in the fire to roast it.

Blake stood at the edge, listening. Waiting.

The girls were moving to the table to fix plates. His family stood in groups, talking and laughing.

Blake had watched Lindsey opening gifts a short time ago. She'd smiled and laughed. She'd loved the jeans that Lucky's wife picked out. Sophie had given her music. Mia, a new MP3 player, without a GPS. Lindsey had opened all of her gifts. She'd thanked everyone. But there was one gift that Blake knew she had been praying hard for. It was a gift only he could give her.

Gage started playing music, a country song about falling in love again. A few feet away Jana paused to listen. Blake walked up behind her and wrapped his arms around her. He leaned to whisper in her ear, and she leaned back against him. "Come with me."

She turned her head and looked up at him, exposing her beautiful neck. He dropped a kiss on the edge of her jawline, breathing in the sweet scent of roses.

"Right now?"

"Right now." He took her by the hand and led her away from the crowd. He avoided eye contact with his grandmother. Granny Myrna had her ways, but this one was all his. He knew what he wanted and how to get it.

They walked along the creek until they came to a place far enough from the bonfire but not too far. Jana looked up, questions in blue eyes that were dark in the fading light of day.

"Blake?"

"Jana." He grinned as he said it and then he leaned to touch his lips against hers. She answered by wrapping those sweet arms of hers around his neck, her fingers touching the hair at the nape of his neck.

He had prepared to say all of the right words, but the words had disappeared the minute she stepped into his arms. He kissed her again, wanting more than anything to sweep her off her feet and carry her away from here. But their daughter was here. Here was the place they needed to be. Tonight.

He explored her mouth, his fingers caressing her cheek, her jaw, then finding themselves in the fragrant softness of her hair.

She pulled back first, her breath soft, her eyes wide. He had to find the words. He had to find the way to make her his again.

Jana stepped back from Blake. The air was cool, and she could hear the swift rustling of the creek a short distance away. The bonfire still blazed, and laughter carried as the girls ate and played.

She listened to the song Gage was singing as he played his guitar. She couldn't quite make out the words. She only knew that she was falling fast, the way she'd always fallen for Blake.

She needed to gather her wits or she'd lose all focus, and she needed focus because she couldn't keep doing this, falling into his arms and wondering if they would ever find a way back to each other.

"What are we doing?" She finally managed something that made sense. Or seemed to.

"We're sneaking off by ourselves." Blake smiled at the response and pulled her close again. "We're rediscovering something important."

"Important?" She whispered the word because common sense had fled again. His touch seemed to send it running for cover.

"Mmm-hmm."

"What?"

He leaned again, brushing his lips across hers. "Us."

She leaned, resting her head on his shoulder. "I've missed us."

"Me, too."

Jana shook loose from the web tangling her heart and mind.

"Blake, we should go back to the party. Lindsey will wonder where we are. And this just confuses everything. It will make her think…"

He put a finger to her lips and quieted her.

"We'll go back in a minute. First, I have to say something."

Her legs went suddenly weak, slayed by the soft look in his eyes, his expression that heated her to the depth of her being. Her heart trembled like the first blades of grass sneaking up to greet spring sunshine after a long winter.

"Okay." The word came out shaky.

"Jana, I love you."

"Okay." This time weepy.

"And I want you to come home, to our house."

"Okay." This time there were tears.

"I'm asking you to marry me again. Be my wife. Be the mother of my children."

"We only have one," she whispered. "And we're already married."

"Exactly. We should have more." He grinned and kissed her again, kissed her lips, her eyes and the sweet spot near her ear. "Marry me," he whispered, sending chills down her spine. "Stay with me forever."

"Blake, what about the lawyer, and wanting to make sure we are as crazy about each other now as we used to be?"

"There is no lawyer. I'm not sure what you're talking about."

"The lawyer called to confirm your appointment."

He leaned, resting his forehead against hers. "Is that why you thought you needed to move, to give us time?"

"Part of the reason."

"Jana, I called the lawyer to tell him to forget the divorce. I admit that it has taken me time to work through what I felt. Loving you and being mad at you, I had to work it out because I didn't want to go back into our marriage still angry."

"And now?" She held her breath, waiting.

"I'm here, Jana, wanting you to be my wife again, wanting you next to me. I want you back in my home, with me, with our daughter. I've had enough separation to last a lifetime."

"Yes." The word slipped out, trembling on her lips.

He reached in his shirt pocket. She held her breath, waiting, and when he opened his hand he held the rings Granny Myrna had told her she had in safekeeping.

Both of their hands trembled as he slipped the wedding ring on her finger, the finger that had been missing that ring for a long time.

"Be my wife, Jana. To have and to hold. Until death do we part."

She nodded and then tears filled her eyes. "Your ring?"

"I'll get a new one."

She looked around, wanting something to make this moment one that symbolized the renewal of their marriage. She took off the ring she wore on her right hand and slipped the pearl ring, her mother's, on his pinky. He smiled as he watched, and heat climbed up her neck into her cheeks.

"I promise to love you forever, Blake. To have and to hold, until death do we part."

"Can I kiss my bride?"

She looked up, her lips parting as Blake leaned to kiss her again. And then he backed away, smiling. "Let's give our daughter the birthday present she's been praying for. Let's give her a family. Maybe one that includes Teddy and Sissy."

She cried then because he was her cowboy, her husband and the biggest romantic she knew. "Yes. Again, yes."

He sent a quick text while she watched, wondering.

"What are you doing?"

"Kissing you again."

He pulled away, smiling as he surveyed the bonfire area. "Okay, all ready."

"Ready?" she asked as he led her back to the fire.

"You'll see."

As they walked back to the bonfire and the group of people gathered together, Tim and Angie turned Lindsey toward them. Gage started playing "Happy Birthday."

Lindsey started to cry and Jana joined her. Their daughter ran to them, throwing herself into their arms. Blake gathered up his wife and daughter and held them close.

"Are we going home?" Lindsey cried into Jana's shoulder.

"Yes, honey, we're going home."

"I love you, Mrs. Cooper." Blake held her in the circle of his arms with Lindsey there with them.

"I love you, too."

They were finally home.

Epilogue

Two Years Later

Jana looked at the clock again. Blake had gone out to check a mare that was due to foal. Lindsey, Teddy and Sissy had gone with him. They'd been gone for two hours. She assumed that meant the mare had given birth. Which was nice for them, that they were in the barn while she sat there alone listening to the wind howl as March went out like a lion, leaving behind four inches of snow.

She glanced at the clock again and went back to reading her book. The door opened. She glared at her husband and children. Teddy and Sissy had officially become theirs six months ago. It hadn't been easy, because everyone wanted Lisa to get better, but Lisa had signed over custody and disappeared.

The four of them, her family, stomped into the house. They were a mess. Their shoes were snow and dirt covered. Blake's shirt looked like the trash, not the washer, was the best place for it. They looked like the happiest family in the world.

She was anything but happy. And she wanted to be. She knew that soon she would be.

"You okay?" Blake kicked off his boots.

"Actually, no, I'm not. You were gone a long time."

"We were just in the barn, Mom." Lindsey shrugged out of her coat and then helped Teddy. Sissy had already hung hers in the closet. "And we have a new foal. He's beautiful."

"You were gone a long time." She looked at the clock again, and this time grimaced and tried to breathe through the pain.

"Jana?" Blake's voice now registered panic that she could appreciate. If she wasn't in so much pain she would have smiled.

"We have to leave now."

"Leave now?" Blake shook his head. "I'm going to make popcorn and…"

Lindsey slugged his arm and headed out of the room. Obviously someone had to be in charge, and Jana had a feeling it would be her almost-fifteen-year-old daughter and not her husband. "Dad, we have to go. To the hospital?"

"To the hospital?" He went a little pale. "Now?"

Teddy and Sissy raced after Lindsey.

"Now, Blake."

"The baby isn't due for two weeks."

"Babies don't always care about due dates. My water broke and my contractions are five minutes apart."

"Why didn't you call me?" He was in motion now, having recovered. He reached for the muddy boots.

"Do not wear those to the hospital. Go change clothes."

"We have to go." He grabbed them and started to shove his foot in.

"No. You are not wearing barn clothes. You're not going to stand next to me in the delivery room smelling like manure."

"I don't..." He lifted his arm and sniffed. "I'll change clothes."

"Thank you."

He sat next to her. "What can I do, honey?"

She growled as another contraction hit and then she smiled. "GET READY!"

"Gotcha." He kissed her cheek and then he was gone. She smiled at his retreating back.

For two years, life had been better than ever. But she was afraid. She knew that Blake was afraid, too. What if she had this baby and slipped back into depression?

Blake returned and his smile disappeared. "Jana, you're okay. We're okay."

"I know we are." She sniffled. "It's just hormones."

"We're going to have a son, Jana." He helped her to her feet as Lindsey came back with her bag. His arms went around her and he nuzzled her neck. She wished it didn't hurt to breathe.

"We should go," she whispered into his shoulder.

"We're going, but you have to trust me. Dr. Almon knows the past and he's going to be monitoring you. And I'm here with you."

"I know." She smiled up at him through tears that were more joy than sadness. "And I do trust you, and I know that God isn't going to let me down."

"Could we go now, please?" Lindsey was at the door and jerked it open. It was still snowing.

"Man, I hope I don't have to deliver this baby in the truck." Blake shuddered and headed her toward the door. He turned off the lights as they walked out and pulled the door closed behind them.

Jana held on to his arm as they walked down the steps to the truck. "It should be warm with spring flowers."

"There are jonquils blooming," he offered. She only nodded because flowers no longer mattered. Another contraction had wrapped around her middle. She hoped he would drive safe but fast to the hospital in Grove. She didn't tell him, but she'd already called his mother.

Two hours later Chance Cooper came into the world, with a slightly pointed head and a healthy cry. Blake held him for a moment and then placed him in her arms. Jana smiled down at the little boy and then at the daddy who would teach him to be a man of honor. And a cowboy.

"I love you, Blake Cooper."

"I love you, too, Jana."

* * * * *

Dear Reader,

When I started writing *The Cowboy's Reunited Family,* I had a specific story in mind. I had the hero and heroine picked out, matched up and the wedding all planned. But fiction, like reality, sometimes takes us by surprise. No matter how hard I tried to make that romance work, it didn't. Some couples aren't meant to be.

It wasn't until I brought Blake's ex-wife back into his life that I found the story, the romance, the perfect Happy Ever After. Blake and Jana, even though the odds were slightly against them, were meant to be.

I hope you enjoy their story.

Brenda Minton

Questions for Discussion

1. After searching for his wife and daughter for ten years, they suddenly return to Blake's life. Blake has to deal with anger, happiness and forgiveness. How does he separate his feelings for his wife and daughter?

2. Jana faces her fear to save her daughter's life. How did those fears affect the choices she made in the past?

3. Jana grabbed hold of faith as a lifeline while facing her daughter's illness. Do you think the faith was real to her in the beginning or did it grow in her as she experienced it?

4. When faced with his daughter's illness, Blake makes several discoveries about his life, his feelings. How do you think he grows during this process?

5. How did a chronic illness change Lindsey's life?

6. The Coopers are a forgiving and loving family. Does that mean they trust her completely now?

7. Lindsey missed out on a childhood in Dawson with her Cooper family. But she lived her childhood not knowing what she was missing. How would she feel about coming back and about what her mother had done?

8. How difficult was it for Jana to face what she had done to Blake and to Lindsey?

9. When did Blake realize he wanted his family back, including his wife?

10. Blake's lawyer as well as Tim Cooper mention God's hand on this situation. How did God work in the lives of Blake, Jana and Lindsey?

LARGER-PRINT BOOKS!

GET 2 FREE LARGER-PRINT NOVELS PLUS 2 FREE MYSTERY GIFTS

Love Inspired

Larger-print novels are now available...